CHASING GORDON

By Timothy P. Hill

*This book is dedicated to all who have
toiled at a weekly newspaper.*

Chapter 1

Another edition of The Harvey Herald was put to bed. Done. Ready for the printer and out of Eddie Bell's hands. The week had gone more smoothly than most. Other weeks it was put to rest or put out of its misery. Today it was put to bed. Amongst seasoned journalists "putting it to bed" was a common expression. In reality getting the paper to press was hardly like going to bed unless a nightmare was imminent. Most of the time it was a painful experience that meant long hours, short tempers and countless mistakes.

With affordable subscription rates, The Herald circulated to nearly 8,000 subscribers in five North Dakota counties and a handful of stragglers in Lodi, California. The newspaper had been published weekly under the same name for 86 years in the central North Dakota town of its namesake. This impressive string continued under Eddie's watch as editor and general manager. The 24-year-old editor managed a news staff of three that included himself, his managing editor and a high school kid who developed the film in the makeshift darkroom—when he wasn't at football practice or an orthodontic appointment. Eddie affectionately called the newspaper "the rag" but scorned others who dared utter the words.

Eddie had no delusions that his lofty title as editor impressed anyone, with the notable exception of his boastful mom. She proclaimed to everyone she knew, with a mother's intonation, what her son did. To have her tell it, her son was the best American writer since Mark Twain. So committed was she in her son's career choice that by the time she wrapped up her salute, she nearly had Eddie believing it. Nearly. "It is an honorable profession," she would say. Eddie was quick with the sarcasm. "So is grave digging." Optimism was not Eddie's strong point.

In college Eddie gravitated toward the sciences because he was told that's where the cute girls were. He thought a career in biology would suit him as well as any. He excelled at cat dissection in high school biology. Cat guts and formaldehyde did not trigger his gag reflex. The tricky part was sliding the stiff feline out of the plastic bag without it sliding across the counter and clunking on the floor like a saucer. That was the extent of Eddie's skills in the sciences. His career plans changed suddenly while Eddie settled behind a desk in chemistry class – the professor was handing out a mid-term exam that completely blind sided him.

Afterwards a desperate search for a substitute major steered him into journalism. Eddie had kept a diary when he was a kid. Most entries could be summed up as, *"Got up. Went to school. Came home. Fooled around."* That was back when fooling around and horsing around meant the same thing with no immoral connotation. *"Had meatloaf for dinner. Went to bed."* The meals would change and the buddies would change. Meatloaf was always a good night. Though a regular regimen of heavy, starchy foods was the reason Eddie was always battling the paunch.

So Eddie figured, based upon his journal entries, he could communicate a story as well as the next guy. Plus, the girls in the journalism department were better looking.

Before graduating he would be the recipient of the department's memorial award for the student who showed the most promise in the profession of newspaper journalism. Apparently, some anonymous benefactor in the journalism department thought Eddie needed something to boost his resume. Truth be told, he did not rule out his mother's hand in the plot. Promise did not translate into employability.

The latest edition of the Harvey Herald marked a personal milestone of sorts for Eddie, who a year earlier had been laid off from a small daily paper located in southeast North Dakota facing hard economic times. The Wahpeton Daily News was really a glorified weekly. While it hit the newsstands seven days a week, the Daily News never published a national news story on its front page. Once, Eddie begged to put a story about Egyptian President Anwar Sadat's assassination on the front page. It was a big leap for the paper and for Eddie. Unfortunately, the only file photo available pictured Sadat displaying a huge shit-eating grin from happier days. It did not fit with the story of a man just assassinated. The story was on the front page and it was what mattered most to Eddie.

The Daily News was his first job out of college. It was also the first time he had been canned from a job. The memorial award from college apparently carried little weight. The publisher of the Daily News summoned Eddie out of a county commission meeting he was covering as part of his regular beat to inform him that layoffs were impending. He was the first to go based on a policy of last hired, first fired. Without hesitation or guilt, the publisher then asked Eddie to be kind enough to finish the meeting. Eddie dutifully complied. He would later tell his employed friends, "I was so caught off guard, I just did what I was told." At the time, he promised himself to never haul around another reporter's notebook. The spiral-bound notebook and a pen were the quintessential tools of the trade. His apartment and truck were littered with the narrow cardboard covered notebooks that opened from the bottom.

The Daily News publisher followed up the verbal send off with a letter of recommendation—of sorts. In it he explained in grammatically challenged English that due to "extrodinary" economic pressures, the paper was forced to terminate Eddie's position. Trying to cushion the blow of impending unemployment, the publisher assured Eddie that he had performed his duties "within acceptable standards." Not exactly what Eddie would call a glowing letter of recommendation. He had busted his butt for the Daily News. Often, he was single-handedly responsible for the entire local content of the paper. Lame words of advice summed up the letter. "If you find it difficult to secure new employment, I suggest you find assistance from job service or file for unemployment compensation." Smug advice from someone who couldn't spell *extraordinary*. Eddie left muttering a few choice, and correctly spelled, words for The Daily News.

Production day at The Harvey Herald was always frenzy of activity fueled by strong, black coffee and frazzled nerves. A pot was always brewing and Eddie guzzled it by the gallons.

His nails were already chewed to the quick and he didn't want to take up smoking. A coffee cup in his hand had a calming effect. The caffeine kept him on his feet, although slightly jittery. The entire staff would pray that no last minute, obligatory story would appear, upset the apple cart, and require a revamping of the front page layout.

Eddie was satisfied with the content of the latest edition. There was only so much that could be accomplished in sixteen pages of black on white. Page numbers would burst, with increased advertising, to 24 or 32 during the holidays or a crazy days business promotion. When the printers were feeling generous Eddie would have a green or blue ink to tinker with to give the paper some color.

The Herald's publisher had inherited the paper from his father. It had been family owned since the letter press days, when inked, movable lead type was impressed upon paper. His blood was in it but not his heart. He was more interested in status than making a statement. A lavish lifestyle—as much as could be had in Harvey—could not be sustained on principle. Marshall Charlesworth was more businessman than newsman. More bottom line than byline. He expected a large dose of community news which amounted to an endless listing of who entertained whom at whose house and what was served. The ladies responsible for composing community news were protective of their work because they were paid by each inch of drivel they scrawled out on paper. The news content was predominately Eddie's responsibility. Eddie took pride at randomly cutting community news to make room for his human interest pieces or a provocative photograph. Unless they were in attendance, nobody would know that *"Betty Johnson celebrated her 70th birthday with family and friends at the Lutheran Church,"* or that *"The Larson Family Reunion was held at Lake Sacajawea."* Courtesy of Eddie, volumes of community news ended up on the newsroom floor, a victim of Eddie's razor blade wielding editing. Marshall bore the brunt of the ire of the local socialites whose bridge club crumpet party soirée was scrapped from community news to make room for Eddie's story.

Technology wasn't advanced enough yet to electronically lay out a newspaper. Production night had its elements of danger. Newspaper copy was hand cut with a razor-tipped device aptly called the X-Acto knife. It was then run through a hand-fed hot wax machine that deposited a thin layer of wax to the back of the paper and seemingly everything else. Eddie had become accustomed to waxed newsprint stuck to various parts of his attire. A telltale sign of his trade was a scrap of newsprint clinging to the seat of his trousers. The news copy was then affixed to blank news pages in areas not otherwise taken up by display advertising. Page layout amounted to random puzzle work each week. As long as a photo or headline was not cut off by the paper fold, the layout was limited only by Eddie's imagination.

The X-Acto knife and hot wax machine were responsible for weekly job-related burn and cut injuries. Eddie wore a visible quarter inch scar on his forearm after impaling himself with his knife when haphazardly swatting at a bee that errantly flew into the newsroom. He miscalculated his swing and forgot he was grasping a razor sharp object in his swinging hand. Three stitches closed the gaping wound leaving a scar worse than the actual injury. Explaining to the Workers' Compensation Bureau how a knife wound was caused by a stray bee was a delicate and embarrassing task. "Yes, I said bee," Eddie told the Bureau investigator. "Yes, I stabbed myself."

Though the work was hard and somewhat hazardous, there was no money in news reporting. The best of writers were paid a paltry wage. The only reward to a journalist was seeing the byline above a colorfully written human interest story sure to be the fixation of every patron at the local cafe over a cup of coffee and a plate of scrambled eggs. Eddie wasn't vain enough to think people really gave a damn. He knew most folks in town wouldn't read past the headline or at best the first few sentences of any story, equipped only with an attention span for community news.

Errors were a whole other matter. If a name was misspelled or a quote taken out of context, Eddie would be cursed the next day and his likeness burned in a proverbial effigy. Eddie had no tolerance for errors either. When mistakes happened no reader was a match for Eddie's disdain for himself. More than once he had threatened to abandon the fourth estate because of a misspelling or a caption that was placed with the wrong photograph. Nothing infuriated Eddie more than a high school drama photograph mistakenly accompanied with a caption about a lunker walleye catch at the reservoir or a photograph of a three-point buck shot last second with a caption describing a police chase. "Drop kicking" a newspaper is darned near impossible. Eddie tried. Mistakes were inevitable. At midnight everything makes sense in the blur of exhaustion.

Those inevitable mistakes weren't always in the newsroom. At the scene of an armed standoff at a rural farmhouse, Eddie wildly snapped dozens of what he surely thought would be prize-winning photographs of law enforcement and the suspect at the scene, until the situation became too volatile even for the press and Eddie was escorted to a patrol car for his own safety. The distraught suspect had barricaded himself in his barn with a bottle of Wild Turkey, his grandfather's loaded 12-gauge shotgun and the—a stereotypical, made for television—threat that no one would take him alive. His unfaithful wife wanted a divorce and he was pleading for reconciliation, by lethal force if necessary. Having risked life and limb, Eddie was already visualizing the accolades at the next North Dakota Newspaper Convention when his photographs would rake in the awards. In the middle of his self-aggrandizement he made the horrific discovery he had neglected to put a roll of film in the camera. All he could do was curse himself. The back seat doors of police cruisers do not open from the inside. The incident ended without incident with Eddie snapping a couple of unremarkable pictures through the car window after he made sure film was loaded in the camera. Instead of going out in a blaze of glory, the shirtless and cuffed suspect was led away sobbing a last request. "Somebody call my wife!" There would be no awards at the newspaper convention.

Just as painful was a college photo shoot of singer Harry Chapin who was performing at the student union complex. Eddie shot frame after frame of Harry while he tried to sing his signature song, "Cat's in the Cradle", drawing an annoyed glare from the gentle singer. For his encore he sang the melancholy "Taxi". His sonorous voice sang out the lyrics, *". . . she was gonna be an actress and I was gonna learn to fly. . .".* Right in the middle of it he erupted sternly at Eddie, "Enough snapping already!" and then went on with the sad song without skipping a beat, *". . .she took off to find the footlights and I took off to find the sky".*

Developing the film later on Eddie discovered he over-exposed every shot and there was not one recognizable photograph. All that aggravation and nothing to show for it except shadowy figures on Kodak photo paper. A few months later a car crash would cut short Harry Chapin's life. The only celebrities he would successfully catch on film were father and daughter country vocal duo, The Kendalls. There were still days when he found himself humming their only hit single, "Heaven's Just A Sin Away." The photos along with the negatives got lost over time. No evidence existed that he took the photographs. Few knew who The Kendells were anyway.

With no glaring errors visible in the latest edition of The Harvey Herald, Eddie was satisfied that everything was in its proper place and promised himself he wouldn't look too closely when the newspaper hit the stands the next day. After all, he had another edition to put out the following week and the following week and the following. There was no dwelling too long on either a success or failure. Each week the newspaper contained a new face, new name, new place and new angle. Each week there were the same errors, the same frustrations and the same exhaustion.

There was still enough time to hit the Ponderosa Bar for a beer and a bite to eat before closing time. The bar served cold tap beer and cruddy frozen pizza and it was the only place open at midnight. A liberal shaking of salt and a generous dose of Tabasco gave the pizza some flavor and some bite and made the beer go down quicker.

Without much persuasion he convinced, Rob Ellison, his managing editor, to join him. They were both single in a town with no available women, so neither had anybody to race home to who might give a damn. Rob was a Minnesota product, raised in the heart of potato country. He grew up at Barnesville, Minnesota where they glorified potatoes and dedicated a week specifically to celebrate the bulbous vegetable. Part of the festivities included mashed potato wrestling and the crowning of a potato queen. He and Eddie had worked together at The Wahpeton Daily News and, like Eddie, Rob had ambitions about being a serious reporter. He had the good looks for television but had more to say than a 30 second spot allowed. When the managing editor job opened at The Harvey Herald, Rob was the first and only person Eddie considered for the position. Rob accepted the job on faith, having never seen the town or the paper. He was easy going, non confrontational and too trusting.

Eddie volunteered on moving day to help Rob relocate to Harvey. With half of Rob's belonging in the back of Eddie's truck, Rob would have to follow if he wanted to get his stuff back. Confidence in his decision dwindled the further they drove and the closer they got to the place Rob would soon call home.

"Where the hell is this place?" He kept checking the map for reassurance and for an escape route. Rob had the sinking feeling he had made a very bad decision. Eddie knew exactly how Rob felt but wasn't about to say one discouraging word. As time wore on, Rob would claim that Eddie's flattering portrayal of Harvey was a deceptive ruse.

Eddie had hired Rob more as a playmate than an employee. Both were disillusioned journalists who had been inspired by the revered Woodward and Bernstein, The Washington Post golden boys, and the irreverent Hunter S. Thompson, the original gonzo journalist. They believed their skills were squandered in the small town where folks cared more about what attendants wore at so-and-so's wedding or what was on the menu at the church bazaar than they were about serious investigative reporting and a tightly crafted story.

They drowned their woes in tap beer and contemplated their future in an alcohol induced buzz; still picking newsprint off their clothing. By the end of the weekly production night they were weak, fatigued and bedraggled. The bottoms of their feet ached from standing on cement floors. Their calves were ready to burst. They had a perpetual tender spot in their lower back from bending over newsprint. Generally they were in a daze after production night. It was difficult to grasp a full mug of beer. They managed. "If I wasn't so tired, I'd be depressed," Rob said reaching for the last piece of dry, curled up pizza. Fatigue and depression were readily exchangeable conditions. Eddie muttered his commiseration. "Another great day for the Fourth Estate."

They were the only ones in the Ponderosa. It had become their practice, a survival technique, to take inventory of the patrons. There was bound to be one guy from time to time, literate enough to read, who didn't like something they wrote and wanted to give them a piece of his mind on the knuckles of his fists. Several weeks earlier an employee of the implement dealership took umbrage over a tongue and cheek article Eddie had written chronicling a gaudy twenty-five foot mechanical ape the dealership decided to purchase and display in front of their building as some sort of a grotesque mascot. "You'll go ape over our inventory!" The advertising ploy was an eyesore and was too much for Eddie to overlook.

Eddie didn't notice the whiskey-filled shot glass whisk past his head and shatter against the wall behind him in a spray of Jack Daniels and glass fragments. He did notice the disgruntled employee and his band of thugs closing in on their table with chalked pool cues in hand. An ass-kicking appeared close at hand. Who knew the ape had such a fan base? "Come on boys, is this really worth it?" Eddie said trying to reason with the gathering mob. The toothless grins of the thugs standing over him answered the futileness of his plea. To reach the exit, Eddie would have to plunge through a gauntlet of blue collars hell bent on mischief, leaving Rob to fend for himself. Fortunately, the bartender didn't want to clean up an unnecessary mess and stepped in the way to diffuse the situation with a round on the house. Being a Vietnam veteran with a bat behind the bar and absolute power over the beer taps, no one would mess with the bartender. "Take it someplace else," was right out of the bartender's handbook.

The beating could wait for another day. Rob had a way of just pissing people off. Strangers had the urge to kick his ass for no apparent reason.

At the same bar on a different night, a couple of drunks intentionally dumped a beer on him and shoved him against a pool table without provocation. A stunned Rob managed a, "What's your problem?" The drunks predicted Eddie's lukewarm reaction and gave him a good shove too, dumping his beer and the rest of their salty supreme pizza on the floor. So inebriated were the combatants it resembled a brawl in a weightless environment. No lip was split, no eye was blackened, no blood was shed. Pride was blemished. Once again, the bartender was there to come to the rescue before things got out of hand and before Eddie and Rob really had to defend themselves. The guy serving the booze with the chipped teeth and tattooed arms became their guardian angel. "Consider some self-defense classes. I may not always be around." They made sure to leave a generous tip.

Mercifully on this latest outing, they were the only ones in the bar, so the assault risk level was low. "Why are we here?" It was a question Rob raised at least once a week since he landed in Harvey and Eddie wondered himself as much if not more. Eddie knew it was not an esoteric question about the meaning of life, although they had those discussions as well. The question at hand was why they remained at a dead end job. The hour was too late and Eddie was too tired for encouraging words. He had no good answers anyway; no morsels of wisdom. "I'll buy us another round," was all Eddie could muster and was just in time for last call. Rob was somehow comforted by the offer. Eddie motioned to the bartender with two fingers raised in the air and another round was on its way.

They had squandered by indecision previous opportunities to move on to greener pastures. A Navy recruiter on his way through town had offered them officer status if they enlisted on the spot. The recruiter had some quota to meet and was ready to hand out stripes. As college graduates they could have enlisted as first lieutenants. "See the world, boys," the recruiter challenged. His uniform was as slick as his pitch to them. Looking around, he added, "Anywhere else has to be better than this." They regretted now that they didn't do it. The Vietnam War was over and there was no major conflict going on around the world that would lead them to some rice paddy hoisting an M16 over their heads. It would have been a ticket out of town and given some closure to Rob's question, not to mention a nifty dress uniform. They talked each other out of a life in the military and instead complained, drank and searched the want ads for other employment opportunities. Rob and Eddie were their own worst enemies.

When the bartender unplugged the juke box and started stacking chairs they knew the time had come to decide who was going to draw the short straw and have to drive the paper 26 miles to the printing plant at Rugby, North Dakota in the wee hours of the morning. The regular courier had come down with a case of the gout and couldn't shift the gears on his pickup. Leland Jones did odd jobs for the paper. He did odd jobs all around town. It got him out of the house and away from the nagging wife of 53 years. He stroked his thick white mustache when he complained about his gout. Deep wrinkles and age-spotted skin were the badges of honor for a man who worked every day since he was sixteen. Leland would miss the drive to Rugby in the morning.

Eddie was exhausted and tempted to pull rank on Rob. Instead, they chugged their beer as they always did, the slower one being the loser and thus the newspaper escort. "Go home and get a good night sleep, Rob." There was still a good swig in Eddie's mug. He was in for an early morning drive with a likely hangover. Rob grinned as he wiped foam from his lip with his sleeve. "Serves you right for dragging me here."

Chapter 2

Rugby, North Dakota is touted as the geographical center of North America. A stone monument has been erected to eternally mark the spot. Notable features in the state, few as they may be, are exploited as tourist attractions. North Dakota adopted George Armstrong Custer despite the fact he stayed only briefly at Fort Lincoln in Bismarck before embarking on his last stand against the mighty Sioux in Montana Territory. Long stretches of farmland dotted with missile silos blanket the state. If the state was cut off from the rest of the country its inhabitants would not go unfed or unarmed.

At five in the morning Rugby was just a place that separated Eddie from his warm bed and a good night sleep. The four hours of fitful sleep was not enough. He worried about not hearing the usually incessant and unrelenting clang of the alarm clock. If that happened the 86 year publication run of the paper might end along with Eddie's employment. He dragged his butt out of bed, stumbled into the shower, and pulled on a sweatshirt and jeans. Although his hair had been receding since college, there was still enough to look ratty in the morning. Stepping into the cold of the morning, Eddie was convinced he was the only person awake in the geographical center of North America, if not the entire Northern Hemisphere.

Slick roads slowed travel speeds and made the drive resemble a funeral procession. The way his head pounded, he felt more like the horizontal passenger in the lead vehicle of the imaginary procession. It was a good thing there was no competing traffic on the roadway. On the prairie plains, on certain stretches of roadways, motorists could find themselves owning the road for miles before encountering another vehicle.

Eddie still drove the puke green Chevy pickup he extracted from his dad so he would have some form of transportation. The odometer clicking its way to 200,000 miles, almost a one-way trip to the moon. Despite the high mileage, his dad parted with the truck reluctantly and in farewell said, "It will get you where you want to go." Eddie wasn't too sure about the endorsement. But then again, Eddie didn't really know where he wanted to go. The old Chevy was far from a chick magnet. It had so much play in the steering wheel that it was difficult to drive a straight line and a true wonder how it ever made a successful turn. On icy roads the faulty steering intensified the hazard. Gritting his teeth and gripping the wheel, Eddie didn't need a cup of coffee to stave away fatigue. The stomach-turning fear of spinning uncontrollably into the ditch kept him plenty alert.

Five competing weekly papers were published on the same day at the same plant. It was survival of the fittest. The Pierce County Tribune was already winding through the press. The Tribune was Rugby's paper so it had the advantage of proximity to the printing plant. The editor of the Bottineau Courant pulled into the parking lot just ahead of Eddie. The Bottineau Courant was a perennial favorite at the newspaper convention and Eddie's biggest competition. The Courant experimented with creative layout and photography and had the advantage of being nestled in the rolling hills of the state where a breathtaking photo was just a point of the camera away. Eddie hated the Courant. It reminded him that The Herald wasn't as good as he thought it was. The Courant editor managed to get his subtle digs in each week. Larry Wilcox was a wiry cuss with enormous flair for writing and photography. His ego was also enormous. Eddie remembered him from college. He was on the verge of graduating when Eddie transferred to the journalism department. His claim to fame was a weekly shopper that contained all advertising and no news content. The idea was an abomination to Eddie. Examining Eddie's paper, Larry would lob non-compliments. "That's a good story. We did the same story a month ago."

It was always a battle who got printed first. Having verified the position and location of all the photographs Eddie gave the go ahead for the run. "If something is wrong now, it's too late to fix it," he said handing it over to the press manager who couldn't care less. He couldn't help but look over his shoulder and see what the Courant was up to this week. Scavenging story ideas from his competitors was not beyond him. He didn't have time to spy too long. Subscribers expected him to return with fresh black ink on newspaper stock. Coffees were poured and the wait was on for the latest community news.

With the paper at the printing plant there was nothing to do but wait. On days when the roar of the web press rollers dragging the paper stock through a series of turns became too much to tolerate he would wait at the local diner next to the stone monument over a plate of rubbery eggs, boot leather bacon and blackened toast. "What'll it be, hon?" Startling Eddie back to consciousness the gruff waitress rummaged in her apron for a pen. Over the years she had waited on too many tables and closed too many bars. She smelled like cinnamon rolls and cigarette butts. Eddie mindlessly ordered the breakfast special without looking at a menu or knowing what he was getting. Coffee with a splash of Half-N-Half would have sufficed. Eddie knew that Rob was at his trailer sleeping it off. "The bastard!" The salutation resonated in his aching head. Looking around he hoped he wasn't talking out loud and scaring the other customers. The only reason he was in Rugby and not Rob was because of his low tolerance for beer chugging. He should have predicted the outcome of that lop-sided contest. More than once Rob easily drank him under the table after a grueling production night. Eddie could only consume so much alcohol before getting bloated. Though when it came to food, Eddie could down a half dozen loaded tacos and a basket of seasoned fries, no problem.

The eggs tasted good. The bacon crispier than normal. The waitress kept Eddie's coffee topped off and knew from years of waiting tables when to leave customers alone. The skill meant the difference between a good tip and being stiffed. The breakfast crowd was heading for the till, the door, their cars and work. The steady exodus was Eddie's cue that the paper run was complete and he should head back to the printing plant. Eddie left a five spot on the table. It was a generous gratuity for him.

With the freshly printed papers wrapped, tied and stowed in the bed of his truck Eddie steered the Chevy back to Harvey and a well-needed weekend of recuperation. Though it was barely noon, he was aching for his slippers and a hot cup of Sleepy Time Tea. "What a life I have carved out for myself," he thought grimly. The sun had reduced the road ice to slush, allowing Eddie to loosen his grip on the wheel and daydream on the monotonous trip back home.

There was something special about a freshly printed paper. The feel of it, the crease in it and the smell from it. On each page there was something to touch an emotion, turn a grin and increase awareness. Like reaching for the center slice of a loaf of bread he would reach into the middle of a stack to retrieve a pristine copy with no curled edges, no crimps, no tears – a virgin copy. Eddie loathed reading somebody's leftover paper; one that's been turned inside out, with coffee ring stains and missing pieces or gaping holes. A fresh newspaper meant a break in the day, a quiet moment in a comfortable chair or on the commode to catch up on what was going on. Every real newsman worth his oats felt the same way. While Eddie had fallen into journalism by a process of elimination and had to work at it, Rob was destined to be a journalist and it came to him naturally. Like every other writer, Rob was looking for the inspiration for the next great American novel. Rob would jot down a word or a turn of a phrase on a deposit slip, a match book cover, a napkin or toilet paper. "You never know when or where the creative juices are going to flow." His pockets were full of scraps of paper. Many a great story idea was lost in his jeans on laundry day.

As an added perk to the title of managing editor, Eddie offered Rob the spare bedroom in the trailer he was renting at the time. With paper thin walls and warped floors, the tenement on wheels was not a show place. Cheap and spacious were the best features. There was a selfish motive behind Eddie's goodwill. He needed the extra rent money. The newspaper business was not cutting it financially. Scrounging for pennies under cushions to buy a burger at the Tastee Freez became a weekend ritual. More than the rent money, Eddie needed the intelligent conversation and in this area Rob's cup runneth over. He was an encyclopedia of knowledge and a closet philosopher. Rob read voraciously when he was sober and pontificated when he was inebriated. Jack Kerouac, Larry McMurty, Robert Persig, Ray Bradberry, George Orwell, Kurt Vonnegut and Tom Wolff were all in Rob's pseudo library and he was quick with quotable references. He preferred quoting lyrics from his impressive vinyl record collection. One of his favorite lyrics was "this town has too many churches and not enough truth." Not too many weekends would go by in Harvey without Rob dredging up that gem of a sentiment. The name of the musicians escaped Eddie, but laughable or not the lyric suited Harvey, home to some 3,000 residents and plenty of churches.

Rob also liked his doobies. Depending on one's perspective, he could be perceived as a pothead or a college professor. A ready stash in a baggie materialized from an undisclosed location around the trailer and he never divulged his supplier. For all Eddie knew, Rob grew it himself. There wasn't a lot to keep a couple of young, lonely bachelors occupied. They tired of dodging shot glasses and bracing against insults at the Ponderosa. It was too exhausting to drive the seventy-five miles to an urban center for a decent meal at a restaurant or a movie at a superplex. Harvey had a movie theatre, so to speak. The State Theatre had a screen the size of a queen-sized sheet. The rows of seats at the State were not bolted to the floor. Too much of a recline and a whole row of theatre goers could end up on their backs. By the time the State premiered a new blockbuster it wasn't new or a blockbuster anymore.

It was just too weird for two straight guys being seen together at the movies and still be thought of as straight. That kind of spectacle just wasn't cottoned to in a small town. It definitely wasn't the type of community news God-fearing, small town folk wanted to read about in their weekly newspaper. Living in a trailer together raised suspicions enough.

When they weren't chasing the news, they would fine tune their skills at rolling joints in the trailer and becoming one with the ethereal, mesmerizing sounds of The Moody Blues. The problem with being stoned was it was only a temporary fix for their depression, loneliness and wanting of something more. There was also the worry that the local cop might be on to them and bust through the trailer door. The cop was a portly fellow who still sported the same uniform he purchased when he still liked his job. They thought they could dispose of any illegal contraband before he made it up the trailer steps.

At a loss for other bright ideas, Eddie thought community involvement might be the answer and an alternative to running from the law. He joined Kiwanis and Toastmasters. Each week he split his time at each club giving persuasive speeches before breakfast and singing patriotic songs before lunch. By year's end both clubs were less one member. Eddie lasted in both clubs long enough to acquire membership certificates suitable for framing. Rob was not a joiner. "I wouldn't belong to any club that would have me as a member."

Typical of most small towns the young crowd was driven away by a search for education, money and careers. Small towns were not a haven for opportunity. People move to small towns to slow down, disappear, or retire. Those that stayed or returned already found what they wanted where they were or didn't find what they thought they were looking for out there. The local photographer was engaged to the druggist's daughter. Jay Smith and Christi Spencer were betrothed at birth, or so it seemed. Everyone knew they were destined to get married. Of course they were high school homecoming king and queen. Their circle of friends was small and select; a consequence of a town that held limited opportunities for people with promise. Eddie and Rob were invited to a few of their parties. Had there been the remotest possibility of anything else to do they would have politely declined. All of their usual guests tended to arrive as couples which made Eddie and Rob feel a little awkward. Being outsiders the inside jokes were lost on them, feeling as much of a novelty as foreign exchange students at a high school prom. Drinks were served, but not strong enough or often enough for Rob and Eddie. Racquetball, investment strategies, and wedding plans dominated the talk. Nary was a word spoken of politics or religion.

A well-meaning Christi offered to play matchmaker. "We have to hook you guys up with some nice girls."

Well aware of the sparse female population within a 20 mile radius, they knew it was an empty promise.

"We'll hold you to it." Eddie said, less than confident of her match making abilities.

Rob was more circumspect. "I'd settle for another beer."

Working together and living together eventually became too much of a toll, plus they were too much of a bad influence on the other. Let alone being paper thin, the walls of the trailer started closing in. They both needed some privacy and a change. Eddie had heard about a rental at an abandoned Christian campus outside the city limits, just far enough to be ominous. The faculty, students and administration had long ago relocated to greener pastures in Bismarck. With a little Pledge, Pine Sol and clean sheets, the buildings were ready for occupancy. There were no outward signs of deterioration by vandals or nature. In the cafeteria remained all the stainless steel pots, pans, plates and utensils, ready for a big gathering. The dormitory buildings were still furnished with beds, mattresses and dressers. In the classrooms, the black boards had lessons scrawled out in chalk.

The jewel of the place was the gymnasium complete with every sports ball imaginable and a ping pong table. Eddie and Rob wiled away many afternoons smashing a plastic ball at each other. Their noise resonated off the walls of the empty gym. Competitive as they were, they kept a running tally of their victories and defeats. Being the trespassers they were, it caused them to always be on the lookout for someone who would catch them racket in hand. When their cavorting was done, they took care to put everything back in its place.

The Seventh Day Adventists dubbed the property as Peaceful Valley. Spread out across 300 grassy acres it wasn't technically in a valley. It was peaceful in a creepy sort of way. Sort of like a cemetery without the inhabitants, living or dead. Eddie signed a lease to one of the vacant faculty houses. He was the only human occupant on campus. It was the rural equivalent of caretaking at the Overlook Hotel from the pages of Steven King's, The Shining. Every so often Eddie would be greeted by one of the draft horses that roamed the property. The old plug of a horse towered over Eddie. Her sheer mass was intimidating. He called her Isabelle as a tribute to his great aunt. The great aunt was a large, affable woman who could play all of the old tunes on the family upright piano that was ordinarily the depository for dust bunnies and photos of nameless relatives. One of her favorites was the 1950 Nat King Cole chart topper, "Fascination". Isabelle stared through her thick glasses at the sheet music while Eddie's mom followed with the lyrics. To help him remember her name, Aunt Isabelle taught Eddie a play on words, *"Is-A-Belle necessary on a bike?"* Each morning Eddie would treat the horse Isabelle with a green apple from the bag he kept by the back door and ask her the same question his aunt asked him.

He furnished the house with the essentials – a lazy boy recliner and an entertainment center, which amounted to a stand with his television, stereo and a Buddha incense burner.

The one thing Eddie's house didn't have was good insulation. When his heating bill exceeded his monthly rent he confronted his landlord by telephone and braced for eviction. Rather than lose his only tenant, the landlord suspended rent payments until spring when heating fuel and electricity were not such a financial stress. Before Eddie discovered the charitable side of his landlord, he would close off unnecessary spaces in the house and dress in layers. The tea pot was always on boil. He kept a roll of duct tape near the sink when the pipes would burst. Duct tape encased the pipes by winter's end.

Eddie slowly rolled into town with the bundles of papers. He didn't remember driving the truck but somehow it self-navigated back to Harvey. There was disappointment in Eddie's eyes and he spontaneously exhaled. At the publisher's urging, Rob was off chasing down a breaking story on stolen farm equipment. Eddie had hoped to sneak him away for a few games of ping pong.

An unwritten policy earned the early rising traveler to Rugby the right to blow off the rest of the day. Problem was everyone else was at work and there was nothing to do. Eddie used the time to drive around waiting for something to happen. Eddie was pretty sure he could write a story on just about anything and anybody. Talk to a stranger long enough on the street and he will eventually divulge something about himself worth knowing. Everybody has at least one story to tell. Some of Eddie's best stories were unearthed by random chance. The guy drinking coffee at the cafe was wounded at the Battle of the Bulge. The Australian girl at the city park was traveling across America on a bicycle. The lady in the grocery store with a cart full of diapers and formula just adopted two infants from Nicaragua. Eddie couldn't think of one damn thing to write about himself. He was a blank page. It was the hazard of a profession dedicated to the lives of others.

Chapter 3

Before the end of the day, Eddie would memorialize the Area Chubby Contest winding down at the Harvey State Bank. Two obese fellows won the prize for losing 30 pounds in six weeks. For this they earned their picture in the paper. They were looking forward to loosening up their belts and bellying up to a steak dinner with all the fixings. The teller at the bank tipped Eddie off to a photo opportunity down by the Harvey Reservoir where a wild duck was frantically leading her eleven chicks to quiet waters. Not content with being a silent observer, Eddie helped a couple of the chicks catch up to the group.

All in a day's work.

Eddie did not have the fortitude or the finances to go bar hopping every night, which loses the appeal when there are only two drinking establishments in town. Except for the bars, Harvey pretty much shut down after 9:00 p.m. Usually, this was when Eddie would catch up on his letter writing and channel surfing. His two favorite dramas preceded and followed production night. The hospital drama, St. Elsewhere, airing Tuesday nights and the police drama, Hill Street Blues, airing Thursday nights. Captain Frank "Pizza Man" Furillo was jumping into the sack with his wife, Joyce Davenport, to discuss the crime operation he had shut down that day. Pizza Man and Joyce ended up in the sack at the end of most Hill

Street Blues episodes. The fictitious character got a lot more action than Eddie. During commercials, Eddie would jot a note to his mother. She was always reminding him to "keep those cards and letters coming". With each line he would reassure her and himself that life was great. No need to worry mom. It was becoming harder finding the bright spot. "Good to be earning a paycheck."

The candor came out in his letters to his best friend, Stafford Ross. Staff and Eddie grew up together in Grand Forks, a university town along the Red River of the North. They went to the same high school and the same church, double dated and cruised around. They fed off each other's strengths, learned from each other's mistakes, dared each other to throw caution to the wind, consoled each other in life's letdowns and praised each other's triumphs. Raised by strong-willed Catholic mothers, naturally they were afraid of everything that seemed the least bit fun.

Shaking off Catholic guilt, they killed more than a safe number of brain cells drinking beer, and exhausted all their emotions dwelling on girls who were leagues out of their reach. They taught themselves a pretty decent version of the Righteous Brothers' *"You've Lost That Lov'in Feeling"* and would launch into it for anyone within earshot. A girl likes a guy who can sing. So they thought.

Staff settled as a loan officer at a small bank in Minneapolis. He wanted to be a fly fisherman. There was no future in dropping a line. Before the move to the Twin Cities, Staff did his own time in a small town. A locally owned bank in Larimore lured him as a loan officer. A local girl who broke his heart caused his departure. Larimore was not so different from

Harvey with the exception that it was 40 miles closer to a city that offered some entertainment.

His voice tended to squeak when he got worked up. Federal Reserve Chairman Paul Volcker was his idol. He squeaked at the thought of him. He heard that Volcker liked a pipe. When Staff started smoking a pipe he persuaded Eddie it was the thing to do. It was the perfect companion to a cold bottle of beer or a hot cup of Sleepy Time Tea. The woodsy smell of the pipe was soothing and the tobacco wasn't going to get him arrested. Holding the pipe in one hand and a pen in the other made him feel smarter. The words on his paper suddenly became more philosophical behind the swirling smoke. Beer letters were more rambling. Tea letters were more poetic.

In the wee hours, Eddie had no one to talk to, or snuggle next to for that matter, so he wrote letters. Staff was his favorite recipient.

"I am celebrating my first anniversary. In the first 52 weeks I have written or contributed to hundreds of stories. Some were good, some sucked. I remember each one – each interview and each hour struggling over the typewriter."

When the tone of his letters changed from hope to despair, from quips to complaints, from banter to bitterness, Staff wagered it was time for a mental health visit.

"Keep that damn horse away from me," Staff warned. Isabelle didn't like Staff. The feeling was mutual. Isabelle would snort and stomp at the dirt at first sight of Staff. Staff would reciprocate with a grunt. Staff liked horses as much as he liked children. And he loathed children. Little kids cowered at his grimace. If they made noise at a neighboring table when he was at a restaurant trying to eat, he would glare at the obviously neglectful parents.

"You just need to get to know her." He wasn't about to let one of his few friends, beast or not, be disparaged.

Staff's eyes widened and the eyebrows raised. "Like hell I will get to know that glue factory bag of bones. I think you have been here too long, my friend."

That exact thought occurred to Eddie on many an occasion.

Staff persuaded Eddie to institute a workout regimen that featured running with no particular destination. Production night beers were showing up on Eddie's waist.

"A healthy body promotes a healthy mind," Staff would say.

Eddie chortled at the irony. "This comes from the guy who smokes a pipe."

There were plenty of stretches of road available for mindless running in the Harvey area. Eddie lacked the stamina and physique for long distance running. What he lacked in natural ability he made up for in sheer determination and will. He went about running as he did journalism. He worked at it. The best part of running was making it to his back door without chucking up a lung.

Staff didn't subscribe to the idea that two guys running down the road in phys-ed issued gym trunks was strange. He also thought it was perfectly acceptable for two straight guys to be seen together at the movies. He was too progressive for small town life. He was too establishment for Rob. They clashed on most topics. One revered Vonnegut. The other

Volcker. They both liked pipes but for different reasons. Eddie played referee.

Sunday nights were the hardest. The frivolity of the weekend was gone and filled by the dread of the week ahead. Weekend guests had gone back to their lives. Sunday nights the world closed in on Eddie. There was no starting or finishing anything on a Sunday night.

Before his mother sent him off to fend for himself, she equipped Eddie with the secret to survival – hotdishes and casseroles. The recipes she tucked in with Eddie's socks were easy to follow and curbed any appetite. With his mother's scribbles as a guide he became proficient at making a decent meal for one. Depending on the contents of his refrigerator he would alternate between tuna casserole and hamburger hotdish. Reserved for the weekends was tater tot hotdish, the holy grail of all hotdishes. He lined the taters in the casserole dish like a mason laying brick. The meals made him feel closer to home. The clattering dishes broke the silence.

The starchy food dashed any benefit his running had gained him. While doing the dishes, he wondered why a guy who could write complete sentences, croon like Bill Medley, and make a palatable hotdish was still washing dishes alone.

Chapter 4

Having been cooped up in his house for the better part of the winter with no real outlet except work, beer runs and trips to his parents for care packages and pocket money, Eddie was suffering from a serious case of cabin fever and had the compulsion to let loose.

It had been an unusually mild month for February with temperatures pushing 50 degrees and barely enough snow had fallen to sweep. The radiating sun and clear sky made it feel even warmer. The local disc jockey was getting ahead of himself playing Beach Boys songs. "Swimsuit weather is just around the corner," the DJ promised as Brian Wilson praised California girls. What better way to celebrate the weekend, Eddie thought momentarily, then to stoke up the barbecue and burn some meat. He caught himself rethinking that assessment. Surely there were better ways to spend an unseasonably mild weekend—skiing in the mountains and chasing snow bunnies, for instance. On his budget though, weekends became the product of affordability. More often than not, the objective was to find something—anything—to occupy his weekend other than obsessing over the week ahead.

In the newspaper business there isn't a lot of down time. Weekends were no exception. Eddie and Rob shared on call duties on weekends which meant that one of them had to carry a battery-operated beeper just in case there was breaking news in the middle of the night or on a Saturday or Sunday. News events happened at the most inconvenient times. The beeper was the publisher's way of alerting them to accidents and incidents. God forbid missing a car crash photo opportunity. Carrying the beeper meant home detention. Leave the geographical range of the beeper and miss a story in progress. A rash decision still haunted Eddie. One weekend night, Eddie got fed up with the beeper and tossed it in a nearby trash bin. The stupidity of the decision was later realized when he was rifling through garbage to retrieve the beeper and battery pack that had popped off. Turns out he missed an impressive garage fire because of his tirade and the misplaced battery. "I had the beeper the entire weekend," he would lie. "Damn thing must have malfunctioned."

Some of the best stories for Eddie meshed leisure with work. Eddie and Rob would brain storm for stories that would combine their desire for loafing with their need to find a passable feature story for the next edition of the paper. One particularly hot summer day they decided to paddle a canoe down the lazy Sheyenne River that wound and twisted through the prairie grasses and farmland in the state. The river may have been lazy but the obstacles along the way were unrelenting. Around every bend they faced and conquered a new obstruction. They spent more time hefting the canoe over rocks and barbed wire than they did paddling in it. Intense sunlight radiated off the metallic canoe while they swatted at swarms of malaria-infected mosquitoes, adding a viral dimension to the trip. Livestock grazing along the banks of the river seemed to find humor out of their misery. They portaged the canoe through algae green slimy mud.

Canoeing 14 miles as the crow flies is considerably longer by canoe. After 8 hours of paddling they lugged the canoe up an embankment to a county highway and waited for the first vehicle to stop that would take them and the canoe back to civilization.

"Don't talk me into anything like this again," Rob complained.

"Quit your whining. This is what we do."

Rob wasn't convinced. "I didn't sign up for this".

"You'll feel better after a shower and a beer," Eddie promised. Beer was the solution for everything.

Not many people are prepared to stop for two guys and a canoe. They finally were rescued by a big guy in a big truck who stared at them like the dumb asses they were. He surely would have a tale to tell when he got home to "the wife". For the next few days Eddie and Rob tended to the sunburns on their faces, shoulders and the tops of their feet.

At risk of their lives, they got their story. The misfortunes and debacles of others have the makings of a good story. With a few eye catching photographs and creative turns of phrases Eddie and Rob made a silk purse out of a sow's ear and it was one less page of the paper they would have to fill. They just hoped their ability to romanticize the trip despite near hospitalization from bug bites and heat stroke didn't encourage someone else to venture down the hellish, unforgiving river. The kid that developed their film dispelled any possibility that someone would duplicate their feat. "And

I thought I was stupid." He grinned widely with his mouth full of silver. Randy Clark hung around the newspaper after school until Eddie offered him a part time job developing film. Randy had a plaid shirt for every occasion and somehow couldn't manage to keep any of them tucked in to his pants. Perhaps, because he didn't keep the pants secured around his waist. Randy entertained the thought of going into the newspaper business until seeing what the job entailed. Eddie figured on taking Randy under his wing to teach him a trade. That is, until Randy burst the bubble telling Eddie he was enlisting in the Navy after graduating from high school.

Ping pong at Peaceful Valley was their follow up feature. Only a couple of plastic balls suffered the consequences for the sake of a news story. It divulged their best kept secret to the world but they were desperate for a story.

Eddie had enough fluff stories stockpiled so he could relax for the weekend. He was happy not being strapped with the beeper for the weekend. He was even happier that Rob had no new hair-brained scheme for a weekend story line.

Desperate to take advantage of unseasonably warm weather, Eddie had bought a tabletop, kettle-style barbecue at the local Pamida. It was a sale item that no self-respecting family man would buy, let alone a seasoned barbecuer! He was dying to break it in before summer. Rob was on his way with beer and brats—libations being his specialty. He was also toting the beeper. The invitation list was rounded out with Libby Mason and her ten-year-old son, Zach. Libby was the secretary at The Harvey Herald and a lifelong resident of the town. Zach was the product of a one-night stand gone too far, as all one-night stands do. The presumed father skipped out. Not about to be shamed, she stayed to face a judgmental population. They were harder on one of their own.

The three of them were within a year of the same age but Libby was definitely the mother figure. She provided the sympathetic shoulder when Eddie and Rob bellyached about long work days, empty checkbooks and dating mishaps. For two hormonal guys, Harvey was a dating wasteland.

"The only available women are married," Eddie would say. They weren't that desperate. Instead, they drank and vented.

Libby was also the mediator for most arguments between the guys and there were plenty. Most resorted to juvenile name calling.

"Speak for yourself butthead," Rob retorted.

"Shut up, hoser." Hoser was a popular putdown although its meaning was somewhat ambiguous.

Handing them both a Budweiser, Libby could defuse any exchange. "Now boys!"

Eddie provided the place. Rob brought the beer. Libby was responsible for everything else. Thoughts of competing for her affections crossed both their minds. She was attractive enough and really the only prospect in town. Her thin frame was accentuated by tight jeans. She was the less glamorous, unpolished version of Farah Fawcett. Knowing she was a rare commodity did not make Libby take advantage of or be taken advantage of because of her position. The fact that she had a son was not a deterrent. She held out for some surveyor who had worked in town on a water diversion project, promised he would come back and hadn't been heard from since. To save face, Libby would remind the guys that Zach was the only man in her life. "You and me against the world."

When they weren't together they all faced their loneliness in their own way. Booze, joints and books were Rob's methods of escape. Libby taxied Zach to baseball, scouts and church. Eddie auditioned for the community theatre play. After a short tryout that amounted to reading an excerpt from the script, he was surprised to be cast in three roles. The high school drama coach was paid a small stipend to direct the community theatre production. She didn't necessarily see in Eddie an acting diamond in the rough. Just not enough men tried out to fill the male roles. Neil Simon's "The Good Doctor" opened to rave reviews from a sympathetic Harvey Herald. Eddie made sure of that over Rob's objections. He took editorial license to hedge the truth. Truthfully the acting was mediocre, the costuming was shoddy and the set design was amateurish. Eddie's mother liked it and gloated over her son. His dad just shook his head. The play got him out of the house and out of his funk.

When The Harvey Herald bowling team was short one member for league play Eddie volunteered. The other members on the team were serious about the sport. They owned monogrammed balls and colorful shoes. They liked to tell Eddie that bowlers "do it in alleys." Not a one could execute a decent sit up or pull up, though they all could launch a bowling ball with deadly accuracy.

Overcoming his phobia of wearing other people's clothing, Eddie selected his shoes from the bowling alley inventory. The only protection Eddie had from the previous occupant of the shoes was the potent disinfectant spray the counter attendant splashed in the shoes before he circulated them to someone else. Fit and color was Eddie's method of ball selection. If his fingers fit the holes and the color was manly, that was good enough. Eddie had no bowling skills. The rest of the team offered no advice. "We wouldn't know where to start." Without bumpers to aid in accuracy his ball would end up in the gutter with regularity. He would redeem himself by buying a round of beers for his other teammates. He ended up buying numerous rounds over the course of the evening. Bowling league night was not so much an exhibition of athletic skills as it was an excuse to drink beer. They had the bellies to back up the beer consumption. The sad thing was that Eddie's inebriated teammates could rack up the strikes and spares. Eddie was lucky to keep the 14-pound ball rolling down the 62-foot lane. He did manage to keep himself out of the lane. The same could not be said about his teammates. The most rotund of the bunch forgot to release the ball from his plump fingers during his swing and ended up tumbling into the lane. He didn't make enough distance to hit any pins. He still managed a spare. By the end of the night Eddie was the only team member capable of driving his own car home.

Eddie's motorcycle got him out of town. The 1982 650 Custom Honda made up for the green turd that was his Chevy truck. It had the speed to put Harvey in the rear view mirrors and put a lot of pavement between them. On the bike there was only the road ahead. A tank full of gas and a stretch of dry payment remedied any sulky mood. The bike was good therapy without a prescription. When he wasn't strapped with the beeper, Eddie would cruise on the bike with no destination in mind. Anywhere would do and there was always something happening somewhere. He got to know a lot of back roads. Things looked better through his helmet shield. The purchase drew another head shake from his dad. "They are only good three months of the year and half of that time it is raining." Eddie guessed that had his dad lived in Harvey he would have had a bike too.

The burgers burning on the grill was the closest Eddie was going to get to summer for a couple of months. Tapping snow off his untied boots, a frosty longneck beer in one hand and a greasy spatula in the other, Eddie watched his friends exchange snowball volleys from the scant snow that had accumulated under the trees and in the sheltered areas. Isabelle observed the goings on but kept her distance. Eddie was glad to call Rob and Libby his friends. Working at the newspaper was like combat, except nobody died. Scuffed up, maybe, but not killed. There was the occasional X-Acto Knife wound. Suffering brings people together.

Rob suddenly stopped and let his compacted snowball fall from his hand. The posture was familiar. The sound that followed was familiar. It was the dreaded beeper. The party was over. Zach expressed what they were all thinking. "Ahhh, ssshit." Libby let the foul language slide because she couldn't agree more.

Chapter 5

News spread quickly about the shooting of two U.S. marshals along a lonely stretch of asphalt near Medina, North Dakota—another small farming community 100 miles southwest of Harvey. The marshals were intending to serve a warrant upon Gordon Kahl, a sometime farmer and a full-time tax protester. They had been tipped off to Gordon's whereabouts and set up a roadblock to stop and apprehend Gordon for a probation violation. The confrontation escalated into a shootout. Rare though it was, fatal shootings were not unheard of in North Dakota. Those instances were more often crimes of passion and not politics. Long winters cultivated deep resentment.

Gunning down two federal marshals at point-blank range was unthinkable. It lasted all of 30 seconds. The body of one marshal laid face down on the asphalt. The other marshal was slumped in his Charger. The FBI commandeered all local law enforcement to undertake a large-scale manhunt of the suspect at large. The suspect on the run was a local man. Many folks knew him, had coffee with him at the local cafe, saw him at farm auctions. Hunting companions respected him as an excellent shot.

Government agents saw a different side of Gordon. To the authorities with warrant powers Gordon was an extremist and a tax protestor. The extreme philosophies of a right wing paramilitary group known as Posse Comitatus made sense to Gordon. The Posse believed that the U.S. Government was anti-Christian and that the highest law enforcement in the country was the sheriff. Before the standoff with federal marshals, not many people had heard of the Posse. People worked hard paying their bills and raising their kids. They didn't have time for politics or protest. Overnight people in the rural state became wary and suspicious and a little less neighborly. It struck too close to home. The Posse was in the heartland.

The tragic event was the story of a lifetime for the two young journalists who had resigned themselves to being hacks who couldn't land a job with a big city daily. It was just the type of meaty story that drew them to journalism. Under the thumb of a publisher who cared more about profits than content and who wanted to be fawned over as he walked down main street, instead of writing articles to educate and inspire, they were reduced to scrap bookers for subscribers. Every time a local kid sneezed subscribers expected a photograph to document the happy day. They were expected to cover every prom night, sporting competition, farm show and ribbon cutting and there had better damned well be plenty of pictures in the next publication or there would be hell to pay. The only news of substance was the school, city and county board meetings. The makeup of the respective boards were comprised of crotchety, retired men, with bulging stomachs, receding hairlines and droning voices, who debated agenda items to death only to table any substantive decision and adjourn to catch the ten o'clock evening news and chow on leftover potato salad in the fridge. Piecing together a news story from the mind-numbing discussions was a challenge. The public's right to know kept Eddie planted in his folding chair. A motion to adjourn couldn't come fast enough.

There was no glossing over the shooting of two marshals. Advertisers and merchants were not happy with the publicity that rained down on their part of the state. Gunfire and bloodshed were not good for local business unless it was deer hunting season.

What benefited Harvey was its distance from larger cities in the state. Consequently, the industry it had wasn't sucked away by the bigger populations. Harvey used to be the county seat for Wells County until folks from Fessenden, a mile down the road, stole the county documents under the shroud of darkness and proclaimed their town the county seat. Old folks in "assisted living" still held a grudge and secretly vowed retribution and demanded reparations.

The main street had thriving businesses anchored by an old-fashioned drug store, a Ben Franklin and a JC Penney's. It didn't seem to bother anyone that the town's main street was Lincoln Avenue and not a street at all. Nobody walked to get anywhere. People hopped in the car to go a block down the street. It took Eddie some adjustment to get used to that practice, but in time he too conformed. The town offered choices. There was a Red Owl and a Super Valu grocery store. Harvey was big enough for two chiropractors, two optometrists and two zealous lawyers who were somehow related. They seemed to settle a lot of their cases. It had a furniture store, hardware store and car dealership. The Catholic Church was an impressive architectural structure. Eddie's mother expected him to appreciate the architecture from the inside. The Harvey High School Hornets were perennially competitive in Class B sports though they always came up short of the championships. It was still Hornet Country. The bleachers in the gymnasium were always full of rowdy Hornet boosters on Friday nights. Eddie even found himself caught up in the school spirit.

The newspaper was at the end of Lincoln Avenue. A town with a newspaper is a town with an identity. Love it or hate it, the town newspaper is what binds and defines a town and gives it a soul. The personality, beliefs, heart, character and prejudices of a town are all revealed in the pages of the newspaper. Eddie was an interloper. As days turned into months the awkward stares stopped and he could walk into the cafe, bank and grocery store without being looked upon with suspicion or distrust. However, he would always remain an outsider.

After being laid off from the Wahpeton Daily News, Eddie blocked from his consciousness the possibility of ever hiring on to another ragtag publication in another one horse town. Between jobs Eddie hunkered down at his parents' house. It was humiliating enough to be laid off. Forced to move back in with his folks because he couldn't afford rent was demoralizing. They were happy to have him until his stay became indefinite and the employment prospects dwindled.

During his unemployment stretch, Eddie wore out his welcome at home. After several months of leeching off his parents, Eddie's dad left his clothes in the hamper to rot, made a racket if he tried to sleep in and cut off second helpings at the dinner table. He would mutter as he put the milk carton back in the fridge. "This ain't no boarding house." A product of the Depression and the War in the Pacific, Eddie's dad was all about self-reliance and picking yourself up by the boot straps. He didn't comprehend self-pity.

Eddie's mother was a little more diplomatic. "Something will come along," she would assure Eddie. But she would qualify her confidence with, "It may not be your dream job," subtly telling Eddie he should take whatever was offered him. Eddie was still her little boy. She never adjusted to the empty nest. Doting on her prodigal son gave her something to do. Joblessness in America reached 10 percent, a rate not seen since the Great Depression. There were a lot of other people sharing his predicament—though maybe not under their parents' roof. President Reagan assured the unemployed that the want ads were full of jobs. Eddie was quite certain the president and former actor had not flipped through the want ads at any point in his life. For those with skills like belly dancing or dealing black jack there was a spattering of jobs. Eddie had compiled quite a collection of rejection letters. It was especially depressing to have a prospective employer, for whom Eddie wouldn't be caught dead working, pour salt on the wound and send him a rejection letter. Living with the parents and relying on them for beer money was not what he expected from his college education.

By the time the Herald job came about Eddie would have taken anything with a paycheck. He had no idea where Harvey was without the help of a map. Located in the dead center of the state it was the furthest most point from every major city in North Dakota. The Herald hired him on the spot. Had it been his nature, he would have been whooping and hollering at the good fortune. Seems as though The Herald was as desperate as Eddie. The departing editor had bounced checks all over town. Town leaders were wondering just what kind of riffraff was working for them at the newspaper. When he left for Harvey there was no big send-off, no congratulations, no party. Eddie was relieved to once again being a productive member of society and not a slug.

The toll of his unemployment shone in his somber outgoing mail to Staff.

"It scares me to see all the people that are getting laid off and to know that I was in their boots only a week ago. It's frightening to think of all the people competing for the same job. I'm glad I found this job. Thank God for small miracles".

After he landed in Harvey he holed up at the Arto's Supper Club and Motel for a few nights until his trailer opened up. Named after artesian wells that were not to be found on any geological map, the motel had a clean room and a heater that sounded like a hovering helicopter. Eddie arrived in town a few days before his start date to get the lay of the land. His first encounter with the inhabitants of Harvey was the front desk clerk, Babe, a silver-haired, spindly woman with a speech impediment she inherited from a bad bout of pneumonia. More a housemother than motel clerk, Babe took an immediate liking to Eddie. Her coffee and conversation were free–both were rich. She didn't trouble herself with the skirmishes and turmoil that erupted in faraway places like El Salvador and Nicaragua. She was aware of troubled places in the world but determined there were plenty of other people, a lot smarter than her, to worry about them. "I'm too old and frail. No one would listen to me anyway." The TV Guide was near for quick reference and Babe could recount the dialogue and plot line for every episode of MASH.

Babe got a chuckle out of a promising young man like Eddie planting himself in a town where nothing happened. "Now what would bring a nice young man like you to this town?" She asked him.

Too embarrassed to tell her that he didn't have anywhere else to go, he stammered something about how the best writers got their start at small town papers.

Babe wasn't born yesterday and wasn't buying the explanation. "You're going to have a hard time finding something to write about." She couldn't have comprehended the storm brewing in rural America.

As news drifted in about the Medina shootings and the story unfolded, the ring of involvement expanded. Gordon's wife had been a passenger in the car and an unwitting accomplice. Their son, Yorie, was there too and was shot in the abdomen. One of Harvey's own sons, Scott Faul was there, in the wrong place at the wrong time. He was on the run with Gordon. Before authorities and his conscience caught up with him, Scott parted company with Gordon. He sneaked home to hug his wife, then surrendered to authorities. Eddie didn't know any of these people. Now his job was to find out everything he could about them. With the shootings in Medina striking so close to home, outsiders took notice and were converging on the town. Harvey and the surrounding area were under a microscope. What residents called the best-kept secret in the state would now forever be linked to one of the most tragic events in the state's history.

Eddie and Rob found themselves in the middle of a story that would garner national attention and were not about to miss out. They did not know who Gordon Kahl was and would never meet him, but before it was all over they would know a lot about him.

Eddie stared at the ceiling waiting to drift off under the rumpled sheets of his bed. He focused on the hole in the ceiling that dripped during every rainstorm. Spring would bring a new season of dripping. A reorganization of his room was in the works so the drip wouldn't be centered over his pillow. His bedroom was in complete disorder. An overnight bag from a weekend to his parents lay unpacked on the floor. A week's worth of work clothes were scattered around the room. Framed pictures and plant hangers were strewn on the floor awaiting wall space. The room resembled a garage sale after a 50 percent markdown. The cluttered space was a metaphor for his life – confused and disarrayed.

Unable to sleep, he drove to the paper to grab some notebooks and film and to collect his thoughts. He was comfortable at the paper. There he had no doubts about his abilities.

The lights in the front entryway were already on.

Rob battled his own insomnia. "What are you doing here?"

"I could ask you the same."

Though they could no longer tolerate each other as roommates, they still considered each other good company.

Rob cracked open a beer from the grocery bag next to him and tossed one to Eddie. "I guess misery loves company."

Come weekend nights in Harvey kids in their souped up cars owned the streets. Cruising up and down Lincoln Avenue, screeching tires, blaring radios and bellowing obscenities was a regular pastime. There weren't a lot of other options. After watching the parade of cars for awhile, Eddie and Rob hopped into Rob's car where a cold six pack of brew was waiting. They drove down to the Harvey Reservoir and dispensed with the remaining beer. Having spent so much time together there was not much else to digest or declare, to expound upon or express. They had even exhausted all likely locations of the artesian wells. A fog was moving in. Morning couldn't come too soon.

"This is big time," Rob said.

"Let's not blow it," Eddie answered.

Chapter 6

Madge was the first one to show at the impromptu meeting assembled by Eddie to organize for the week. A story this big needed everyone's cooperation. Madge Hoffman ran the front desk, renewed subscriptions, answered the phone and placed ads. She was an institution at the paper and had been there as long as anyone could remember which was a surprise because the paper was her biggest gripe. When she wanted to put emphasis on a statement she liked to point her crooked index finger. Madge's son, Cliff, was perpetually in college on the government dime and was the pride of her life though he'd never held a nine-to-five job. When exactly he attended college was a mystery because he always seemed to be drifting into the paper. They appeared to dress from the same drab thrift store wardrobe and sport the same androgynous hair style. Despite of, or perhaps because of, her quirks Eddie developed a real kinship with her. She challenged everything Eddie held true about religion and politics and made him defend it. He braced for an argument every time he walked through the door. A devious wink of her eye and Eddie knew the debate was on.

Madge was an invaluable source of information. No one was safe or exempt. She had the goods on everyone in town and a sharp memory to go with it. Gordon was not an acquaintance but she knew people that knew him and would extrapolate information that would give the stories additional substance. Every patron coming through the door was victim to her sarcastic barbs. "He's as screwy as a two dollar bill," or "She's the biggest slut in town."

The aroma of coffee wafted over Eddie as he pushed through the front door of the Herald. Madge smiled at him over her reading glasses and hoisted her mug in greeting before taking a cautious sip. She had already dug through the newspaper archives to find a Letter to the Editor Gordon had penned two years earlier. The newspaper had a library in just the academic sense. Madge clipped and cut articles that mattered to her and stored them in a four drawer metal filing cabinet next to her desk. She tangled with anybody meddling with her cabinet.

Waiting for the rest of the staff to arrive, Eddie read the pontifications of the man who had so far eluded law enforcement. Gordon quoted the Bible, the Constitution and the Communist Manifesto. He believed he was a warrior against Satan. Gordon seemed to have a premonition that his life was on a collision course with the powers that be. *"What I know about Satanism, makes me not only a thorn in their sides, but a constant threat to their world conquest, and they will stop at nothing to bring about my exit from the world."*

Nothing good could come out of this way of thinking, Eddie thought. And nothing did.

There was no expectation that his typesetter would show for the meeting so Eddie wasn't surprised when Jessica Thorson called to say she wasn't coming. The invitation was extended to her to join the meeting so she wouldn't feel left out though there was no real reason for her to be there other than to spare her feelings. Jessica was the wage earner of the family. Her husband had a hard time holding down a job because he had a hard time showing up to work and a harder time showing up sober. Jessica was a heavy girl, the product of idleness and consumption. The weight contributed to hygienic deficiencies which became olfactorily pronounced after the end of a grueling production night. Her form consumed her chair and the chair was never occupied if she wasn't on it. A lingering odor guaranteed that Jessica's chair would always be reserved for her use.

Adding to her physical problem, Jessica was pregnant. What she thought for months was indigestion was actually morning sickness. Automotive, financial, plumbing, marital and pregnancy were just some of the problems Jessica rattled off as excuses for her no show. Reading Gordon's letter, Eddie was only half paying attention to Jessica on the other end of the phone. He thanked her for the call and hung up on her in mid excuse.

Most of what Eddie wrote was feel good stories. Eddie had a knack for making people come across better than what they thought about themselves. One such story tracked the ambitions of presidential and senatorial candidate, Harley McLain of Eckelson, North Dakota. McLain lived on a 70 acre organic farm in a geodesic dome with his dog, McBean, and his cow, Frank. Like Gordon, Harley did not believe in taxes. *"It is involuntary servitude,"* he would say. Harley believed in peaceful solutions. *"A government of spirit becomes the people. Decisions would come out of the hearts and minds of the people."*

He advocated creativeness over violence and discourse. *"The government is not one that takes from the people but one that puts creativity into people – a government of spirit not of restrictions."*

It mattered little to Harley that at 29 he was not eligible to run for president or the senate. It was the message and not the mission that was important. Eddie was still in college when he crossed paths with Harley McLain. The encounter and subsequent story resulted in a 16th place showing in the national William Randolph Hearst Feature Writing Contest. For a cub reporter an award connected to the newspaper giant meant something. In a turn of irony, McLain later was credited with a song sympathetic to Gordon.

It was not a feel good story that Eddie was assembling the Herald staff to discuss. Gordon was very pragmatic about government and taxes. He believed that taxes were the second plank of the Communist Manifesto and that tax collectors were the *"tithing collectors for the Synagogue of Satan."* What would come to print would be dark and grave. Definitely not feel good.

Vern Thompson made a beeline to an ashtray. He didn't like taking orders from Eddie but begrudgingly showed because nothing happened without him hovering about. What he did at the paper was somewhat of a mystery. His title was production manager. Basically he floated around the production room and took smoke breaks. He was pissed off with someone or something most of the time, stomping around and cursing past a cigarette clenched in his teeth while sweeping his Vitalis slicked hair from his face. A production night would not be complete without Eddie and Vern locking horns.

Vern resisted change. "We don't do things that way."

Eddie first tried to compromise with Vern. "Let's first try to do it this way." As time went on Eddie stopped listening and Vern stopped complaining.

Sharing Vern's grumpy demeanor was his smoking buddy, Laverne Peterson. Vern and Laverne had the same cross outlook on life and the same taste for Camels. Saying their names in tandem always made Eddie chuckle, like they were some long-ago, washed-up comedy duo. They didn't appreciate Eddie's humor though.

Laverne had a chronic hack and spoke with a nicotine rasp. She couldn't finish a sentence without coughing up phlegm. To them, Eddie was just another punk passing through. One editor did things one way, his replacement another. They were there first and they'd be there long after he moved on to greener pastures. What was his training ground was their end of the road. When the pair were off in a corner smoking, Eddie figured they were cursing his name with each puff—at least they were out of the way. In the end, not much would change—Vern and Laverne would still be dragging on their Camels while tolerating another, in a long line of editors.

Eddie carefully folded Gordon's letter and handed it back to Madge for safekeeping. Madge was a little out there but she was reliable and faithful. She held onto the letter until the FBI seized it as part of its ongoing investigation. The agent who relieved the Herald of ownership of the letter wouldn't touch it. He had Madge slide it into a baggie careful not to leave his own imprint. If fingerprints on the letter led to culpability, everyone at the Herald was a suspect.

It was Valentine's Day. The irony was not missed coming just a day after the massacre at Medina. The day would have otherwise have gone unnoticed by Eddie except his mom always sent him a sappy card signed with a question mark in her hand writing. Not only was it a little creepy getting a Valentine card from his mom, it illustrated how pitiful his social life had become. Madge had a handful of cards displayed on her desk. Eddie was happy to be preoccupied with something other than why he had no one to send a Valentine.

Last to show was Rob and Libby, who strolled in laughing about something. Their levity stopped when they saw Eddie wasn't in the mood. He was also a little put out that he wasn't in on the joke, and it made him wonder where Rob went after beers the night before.

"Lighten up buddy," Rob said.

Eddie couldn't believe Rob wasn't taking this more seriously. "This is no laughing matter." He also couldn't help but think how seriously he might be thinking about Libby. If something was going on they weren't talking and Eddie had no proof.

Eddie had the key to the publisher's private party room connected to the newspaper. To punctuate the importance of the meeting he decided to hold the meeting there. The room was paneled in knotty pine and covered with trophy kills. A prized, large-mouth bass hung over the bathroom door. The last time he was in the party room Eddie partied a little too much and accidentally knocked the bass to the floor, the impact separated the slack-jawed head from the body. In an act of desperation, Eddie shoved a yardstick into the body cavity and delicately balanced the head on the protruding end of the stick and hung it back on the wall. Eddie's makeshift surgery was holding up pretty well. The room had an unstocked bar. The publisher knew well enough not to leave expensive liquor out in the vicinity of working journalists. Everyone took a seat on the rustic leather furniture.

"This is nothing like we have ever covered," Eddie said. Complain as they may on a daily basis, there was no arguing this point. He did his best to assume leadership sounding as commanding and deliberate as he could.

Assignments were divvied out. Eddie and Rob would handle all the hard news. Madge would field all calls. Libby got a head start on community news and the regular features – ag roundup, gardening tips, engagement news, obituaries. Vern would hit the streets for ad calls. Their job functions were no different from any other week. Everyone needed confirmation that their roles were important. Even though Eddie and Rob's names were on most of the articles, the rest of the staff was guilty by association.

Marshall unintentionally cut the meeting short. His appearance made Vern and LaVerne scramble for the quickest exit, disassociating themselves from the other hooligans that busted into Marshall's private sanctuary. Eddie showed no guilt. Before leaving the room, Marshall offered his one piece of advice. "No gory pictures, Eddie."

With all the excitement of the night before Eddie had neglected his weekly laundry ritual. Eddie dragged his laundry to work with him, so he would have fresh clothes for the week, and because the 24-hour laundromat closed at 8:00 p.m. There wasn't enough business to keep it open 24 hours. It was so underused, that no one saw to it to give it a name. The sign over the door just said "Laundromat." Most nights Eddie had the place to himself. Rather than watch his underwear tumble dry he thought his time better spent at the newspaper a block away.

He owed Staff a letter. Staff had applied for a job at the Federal Deposit Insurance Corporation. Auditing the activities of other banks appealed to him and thought it would put him on the fast track to the Federal Reserve and that much closer to Paul Volcker.

"I am down at the office typing this letter while my clothes dry. You'll be interested to know I am not wearing underwear as I have none clean. I am wearing pants, however, so not to worry. I suppose you heard about the shootings here. Finally, I have a story to sink my teeth in."

Chapter 7

A heavy, white fog reduced visibility on the road to just a half dozen car lengths. Combined with snow-dusted ditches it was hard to get a bearing on their surroundings. Nothing much distinguishes the landscape once the crops are off the fields. When the white stuff settles on the barren fields every road and every intersection looks the same. It didn't help that Rob and Eddie were in unfamiliar territory. They hadn't been in this part of the state before. Not even by motorcycle. They hadn't covered a story of this magnitude before. They wanted to get an early start to capture their angle of the story that had gripped the state. The shooting of the two U.S. marshals had dominated the coverage on the front pages of every paper in the state and led the major network news. The Governor ordered flags across the state flown at half staff to honor the fallen marshals. The Harvey Herald wouldn't go to press again for two days. Fearing the story could be over by then, they weren't going to spend another minute being on the sidelines.

News leaked that law enforcement were going to converge on Gordon Kahl's home at Heaton, North Dakota where he was believed to be holed up for a fight. Armed with only their cameras and notebooks, Eddie watched the road and Rob watched the map. Both were on edge fearing that they might find themselves face to face with Gordon. They didn't know the man. They knew from the pull of a trigger he had gone from a grandpa with pictures of his grandchildren in his wallet to a man with blood on his hands. The word was that Gordon had pledged to kill as many law officers as possible before being killed himself. What would two gonzo journalists of no consequence matter? They held their breath every time a suspicious car approached or passed. Rob was already ultra sensitive and easily startled. Normally, Eddie got a kick out of jumping around corners and busting through doors to get a rise out of Rob. He didn't dare test Rob's nerves on this trip.

The regulars at the coffee shop seemed to have all the inside scoop. Before the second cup of joe was poured the rumor mill was in full churn. Gordon had a cache of food and weapons and other military supplies stashed in his house. He had carved out a system of intricate tunnels under his house. There were multiple deadly booby traps set for intruders. The speculation was rampant and enough to make Rob and Eddie jumpy.

The truck radio broke the silence and eased the tension. Rob tuned in to the oldies channel. The Mamas and Papas were California dreaming.

The last time they took a road trip they were driven by thirst. A St. Patrick's Day radio promotion at the end of an especially late production night gave them a second wind for a road trip to Fargo. Driving seventy-five miles is not much of an imposition for the promise of free bloody marys. In the wee hours of the morning there is not much traffic on Interstate 94 which is good when eyes are glazed over and heads are fuzzy. Had they lives beyond the newspaper, driving to Fargo for green colored scrambled eggs and alcoholic beverages would have seemed a little wacky. As it was, the trip made perfect sense. Pub promoters hadn't planned for the two early customers. They got their bloody Marys, but the eggs were still the same color the chicken produced. The manager hadn't shown up with any green dye. Eddie and Rob toasted St. Patrick's Day with Mary. Spontaneous road trips are about the destination not the return drive. They are better unplanned and unscripted. There is no doing the same one again.

A news helicopter hovering overhead jolted them upright, the kind of posture when bracing to collide with a deer on the road. Credence Clearwater Revival was warning of a Bad Moon Rising when Rob turned off the radio. Reminiscing about happier road trips would have to wait. The helicopter was a telltale sign that that Gordon's home was close. Helicopters were not a common tool employed by local news media. If there was a helicopter in the air over North Dakota it usually meant someone needed to be airlifted to a medical facility.

Taking no chances, Eddie checked his camera again to make sure it was loaded with film. There was no room for bush league reporting.

"Are you ready to go?" Eddie said turning to Rob.

"This is what we got into journalism for, man."

Eddie found himself being overly cautious. "Don't do anything stupid."

The approach of Eddie's green Chevy caught the attention of a skittish Wells County Sheriff Deputy who was sitting in his patrol car cautiously sipping his convenience store coffee. Someone with more authority placed him far away from the action down the road. From the looks of his midsection, he was in no condition to be in the middle of the action. He immediately flipped on his service lights momentarily blinding Eddie and causing him to swerve. Eddie pulled over the vehicle not wanting to become a victim of a nervous and trigger-happy deputy. Hoisting up his gun belt he cautioned Rob and Eddie to go no further. They flashed their press credentials. He wasn't impressed. "Sorry boys, I can't let you through." He assured them that it was for their own safety. They nodded to feign attentiveness and promised they would be no trouble. They were close enough to get a bird's eye view of the action through a telephoto lens. Gordon's house was small, hardly noticeable from the road. There wouldn't be many places to hide inside. Houses just like it were scattered every 80 acres or so. In this part of the world the closest neighbor can be a mile away. With such isolation fringe ideas can take hold and take over.

A few scraggly goats and chickens darted around the property sensing an impending danger that had nothing to do with dinner. The livestock looked like they had been neglected for some days, probably because their owner was preoccupied with more pressing matters.

At that particular moment there was no place else where Eddie and Rob wanted to be. They weren't the only ones who felt that way. An armored personnel carrier lumbered by on its way to Gordon's house. When the driver saw Rob and Eddie snapping pictures the vehicle suddenly halted. The hatch flew open and out jumped four gung-ho members of the Devils Lake National Guard. It was the first time they had gotten the tires dirty on the armored personnel carrier other than training exercises and they wanted to memorialize the event. The two reporters were happy to oblige. Resembling a class reunion at an awkward mixer, the guard members posed in front of the armored personnel carrier, arms around each other's flak jacketed shoulders, rifle stocks propped on their hips and K9 dogs barking at the end of leashes.

Rob gathered names of their photo subjects while Eddie changed the film in his camera and snapped off a few dozen more quick shots just to be sure he had something to develop. When the armored personnel carrier rumbled away, Eddie noticed that the deputy had also moved on, unable to remain on the sidelines. They took this as an opportunity to move closer on foot to Gordon's house so they would be in a better position to report on what happened without unwittingly becoming part of the story. Representatives from federal, state and county law enforcement had converged at the Gordon Kahl property outside of Heaton, North Dakota. The FBI, ATF, Jamestown SWAT Team, Wells County Sheriff and the Devils Lake National Guard had all focused on Gordon's house. They were ready for a show of "shock and awe" well before that phrase was even popularized.

Even from their vantage point, Eddie could feel the charged atmosphere. Uniformed officers were crouching, running and pointing and they all had gun barrels fixed on the house. The man thought to be inside was somebody's grandfather and now was a fugitive from justice.

A flurry of activity erupted into a barrage of tear gas canisters and a hail of gunfire that peppered the modest rambler, filling it full of holes and smoke. Eddie and Rob were caught between taking pictures and taking cover. The crackling of gunfire was an adrenalin rush. "Holy crap," Eddie said scurrying on his hands and knees to avoid becoming a stationary target for a ricochet. Rob huddled in the ditch peering over when the shooting stopped. "I've seen enough." A goat leaped suddenly over his head and down the ditch trailed by a couple of chickens. They had the sense to get away.

There was no bad shot, no bad framing and no bad angle. Only a botched film development could be their downfall. Capturing the action in front of them was a matter of shutter speed and not creative camera work.

When the shooting stopped Rob and Eddie ran to the truck like a couple of hightailing shoplifters with a lifted soda. Still reeling from the show of force they had just witnessed they stashed their film under the seats fearing that it might be confiscated.

Dozens of tear gas canisters and thousands of rounds of gunfire pierced Gordon's home. A lot of rounds went in. None came out. He wasn't there. The house was empty. The farmer had slipped away. One discouraged officer summed up the day. "We're back to square one."

The adrenalin rush clouded the danger they had risked for the story. For the first few miles neither said a word. Their minds were racing, filtering the events that unfolded in front of them. "There will never be another chance to cover a story like this," Rob said.

Eddie nodded in agreement. He knew Rob was right. As long as they stayed in Harvey this type of news was not likely to repeat itself. North Dakota is not fertile ground for Pulitzer

Prizes. The Fargo Forum won one in 1958 for its coverage of a horrific and deadly tornado. Twenty years earlier, The Bismarck Tribune nabbed a Pulitzer in 1938 for its series of articles about the Dust Bowl. Natural disasters brought national attention to the state.

Eddie's mom called him that night like a worried mother would. There was endless coverage of the shootings on the television. "How goes it?" she asked on the speaker phone so Eddie's dad could hear. The Champagne music of Lawrence Welk was faintly audible in the background. "Same old, same old," Eddie replied. He didn't tell her how close he had been to the action. She would have to read about it in the paper like everybody else. He promised her he was fine and would be careful.

Eddie's head was still racing when he finally fell into his cushy Lazy Boy. He had mixed himself a gin and tonic and tossed in a couple of green olives skewered by a toothpick. Enjoying the evergreen aroma of the drink and kicking off his smelly sneakers, he reached for the unfinished letter to Staff. *"Rob and I were on the scene of a siege at Gordon Kahl's home today. He wasn't there. It was an impressive showing of firepower nonetheless. If you talk to my mom, don't let on that I have been this close to the action. Speaking of action. Are you getting any?"*

Chapter 8

The banner headline would be "Kahl Focus of State Manhunt". The headline was written before any of the stories. There was no cleverness in it. The words fit across the page and conveyed the contents of the story to follow. There would be no play on words. No gimmicks. Banner headlines used to be reserved for the end or beginning of wars and presidential inaugurations, assassinations or resignations—the bigger the headline, the bigger the news. At a young age Eddie would salvage from the trash those daily papers with the big, bold, black headlines. He didn't always know what the story was about but he knew it was important. Newspapers measure headlines by point size. A seventy-two point headline, at about an inch in height, caught the attention of the reader and hopefully one with some loose change in his pockets. The events of several days ago mandated a large point headline.

The Harvey Herald had one of only a few known photos of Gordon Kahl, published when Gordon had first made his political philosophies public. Gordon was sitting on a sofa with his hands resting in his lap. He wore an International Harvester hat slightly tilted and overalls, common among men his age. He stared straight into the camera with an ominous grin. At that time he was not considered a threat to society. Eddie had been fielding calls all day from incessant news organizations scrambling to get a copy of the photograph.

With pride he gloated at The Harvey Herald having one thing over Time Magazine, The Associated Press and United Press International. It had the most recent photo of Gordon and they wanted their grubby hands on it. Eddie made a deal with Time permitting use of the photo so long as little old Harvey Herald was credited for the photo. It only occurred to him too late to ask for compensation; the product of years of not profiteering from fortuitousness.

Rob was in the darkroom helping Randy crop pictures from the raid on Gordon's farm. Eddie may have been Randy's boss but Rob was his mentor. Randy hung on everything Rob said. The darkroom was the classroom and the lecture was on. Randy thought Rob knew everything and Rob liked to think he knew everything. The dark room had a revolving door that kept the dark in. Walls were painted black and a red light dimly lit the room. Pictures were exposed on film paper, brought to life in the pungent developing solution and hung to dry on clothespins. All the pictures were black and white. They didn't have the time, the equipment, or the skills for works of art. Although, one time Eddie thought a good wildlife picture could be great with a full moon. A quarter placed strategically on the photo paper when it was exposed to light did the trick. A bright clean spot was left on the paper where the quarter had laid. Rob often hid himself away in the darkroom to avoid some of the more tedious tasks of production night. One of those jobs was choosing border tape for pictures and columns. Borders came on sticky rolls, like Scotch tape, and in a variety of widths and designs. After going through dozens of picture negatives he and Eddie had narrowed their favorites to three photographs for the front page that would best portray that foggy day when gunfire erupted at the empty house. One of those pictures was the armored personnel carrier and its gun-toting occupants. The picture of Gordon would also figure in prominently on the front page.

Staring at his typewriter Eddie waited for the words to come. Unfortunately production deadlines did not wait for inspiration. Eddie flipped through his notebook from the follow up interviews he was able to secure with impatient law enforcement and cautious neighbors at the scene. *"Law enforcement was back at square one after a two day stakeout that yielded no results in the search for Gordon Kahl suspected in the shooting of two U.S. marshals and the wounding of four others in a standoff Sunday."* It was a satisfactory open sentence though it exceeded the 25 words which he was taught in journalism school as the benchmark for sentence structure.

He paraphrased statements that he wasn't able to write down word for word and credited statements with quotes that he was able to decipher from his own version of scribbling shorthand. Eddie long ago learned never to wait more than a day to decode interview notes, otherwise he couldn't even read his own writing or possibly reconstruct what was said. When that happened he felt like a paleographer deciphering some ancient writing and it got him in hot water.

There was no smoothing over a "misquote". More than once Eddie had to suck it up and eat the words he had attributed to someone else. P.T. Barnum of circus fame is credited with saying that he didn't care what was said about him so long as his name was spelled right. Turns out people do care about what is printed as their words. Sometimes living by the pen leads to dying by a sword. Bracing against the wrath of a reader berating a story was the equivalent of falling on a sword. From time to time someone who felt mistreated by Eddie's pen would give him a piece of his mind by telephone. The worst of it would be the phone slamming down at the end of the one-sided conversation. In those instances, Eddie just kept his mouth shut and let the incensed caller take his pound of flesh. He had grown thick skin courtesy of the newspaper business. One reader who took particular offense to one of Eddie's unfortunate butchered quotes wanted Eddie to remember in perpetuity the mistake. Chasing Eddie through the newsroom, maligning him along the way, he shouted at Eddie whether he liked "shooting from the hip." Attempts at civility only fueled the spectacle. Eddie just had to take it and let the guy burn out.

Eddie did not want any of Gordon's armed cronies chasing him around the newsroom. As he wrote his story he read each word, of each sentence, of each paragraph to get it right.

Over the top of his cushioned cubicle Eddie could hear the girls chatting away while typesetting news copy. Libby had taped Zach's baseball picture to her monitor. Jessica taped her unborn child's ultrasound photo to her monitor. They separated themselves from the stories they were typesetting preferring instead a discussion about the difficulties of parenting. The girls typeset the copy to fit the news columns. They were the last defense to make sure words were spelled right and things made sense. Eddie settled back in his chair.

The story was coming together. *"A stolen 1971 Mercury was found about a mile from the Kahl farm."*

He was used to disruption and distraction when he wrote – the phone ringing and people chattering. There was even the occasional wadded, flaming ball of paper lobbed into his cubicle by a prankish Rob. Eddie was always ready for an assault on his cubicle.

Vern had made last minute rounds to the grocery store, hardware store and drug store to pick up the weekly camera-ready advertisements. For the moment they had a truce. Eddie was grateful that Vern stepped up to take care of the last minute advertising. He didn't want to waste his time double checking that the spiral ham was sale priced or the shampoo was two for one. Laverne was setting ad copy. There was no magic to it. Ads started on the bottom of the page and went from biggest to smallest up the page leaving some room for news copy. The biggest challenge for her was keeping ashes on her lip-dangling cigarette from dropping onto the ad copy.

Writer's block was a common malady. Fighting through the block was a weekly endeavor. If the flow of the story stalled, panic would envelop Eddie and he would have to regroup. The creative juices were flowing. This story flowed from his notebook to his head and to the typewriter. Eddie zoned out the distractions and zoned in on his story. *"Reports of up to 40 shots around the Kahl residence were refuted by law enforcement."* Eddie knew a lot of lead went into that house. The electric Coronet typewriter hummed as Eddie clicked away at the keys. With the press of a finger the keys snapped against the blank sheet of paper. His fingers were nimble and accurate enough to find the right keys and keep up with his rambling thoughts. His typing skills germinated in high school when he realized he could pound out a hundred error free words in less than a minute. Mastering the typewriter at sixteen made him somewhat a clerical prodigy, though he treaded on geekdom. In journalism the skill came in handy. He was Zen with the typewriter keys.

Breaking news interrupted the music playing in the production room. Gordon's wife gave a tearful plea for her husband to surrender without further bloodshed. The next line of Eddie's article was written. *"With a tearful plea Kahl's wife begged him to surrender."* Eddie was in his element, completely comfortable in his ability to communicate a story to the casual observer. Cover the "who", "what", "when", "where" and "why" and start with a catchy lead paragraph and toss in a few quotable quotes. It was the formula to a good story.

"Police vehicles and onlookers lined the county road to catch a view of the action."

His communication skills didn't translate well in self promotion. Searching for a Thesaurus in his desk drawer he came across the rejection letter dated a year ago from the state's only law school. Eddie never read past the "We regret to inform you . . ." first sentence of the law school embossed stationary before he placed it back in its envelope. It was a low point, a closed door. The worst part of it all was that he wasn't sure he wanted to be a lawyer in the first place. It was a way out of the boredom and monotony. It was a way to capture that elusive "promise" that he was to have realized after college. There was no dwelling on the past today.

"A news helicopter buzzed the area." Eddie checked his notebook making sure he used all the relevant quotes.

Eddie had Rob proof read his story while he finished off a day old jelly roll somebody left next to the coffee pot. A proof reader is the bane of existence to a self respecting writer. Rob and Eddie had an understanding that they would only spot and point out grammatical and spelling errors and would only suggest the rewriting of paragraphs without imposing their style.

The newspaper was full of farmland foreclosure notices. Hard economic times were forcing farmers off land that had been in the family for generations. There were a lot of desperate folk out there. Some sympathized with Gordon and turned him into a martyr for the plight of the farmer.

Eddie laid out a couple of pages of community news, the want ads and the legal notices. Technology was not advanced enough to computer generate a newspaper spread. The technology available at their disposal was hardly affordable to a weekly newspaper running on a shoe string budget. Eddie and his staff took the typeset copy, ran it through the wax machine and manually assembled it page by page. Working off waist high slanted light tables not only facilitated the layout but kept them awake during the long evening.

The final product was the culmination of a week's worth of leg work and one night of frenzied paste up. Satisfied that stories continued to another page led the reader to the right jump page instead of leaving them hanging with an incomplete ending, they stacked the completed pages in numerical order and called it a night.

By the time they deposited themselves on bar stools all the ash trays were steeping with butts and all the frosty mugs were room temperature and lip marked. Life at the bar was filtering to the street before they could make it through the door. It was one of the occupational hazards of their trade. The party was over before they could get there because they were off covering someone else's life for the pages of the paper. By the time they found their second wind the other bar regulars were either pooped out and ready to hit the hay or worked up and ready for a romp in the hay.

Always the one for ceremony, Eddie raised his bottle to toast another paper put to bed. No one could say that he didn't appreciate the reliance he had on his friends to get the paper out week after week. Rob and Libby had come to expect beer induced, but heartfelt, platitudes from their reluctant boss. Beers go down faster nearer closing time.

On production nights Libby's son stayed with her mother. Not having to race home to relieve a babysitter, it was her time to live a little and drink irresponsibly. Anyone who was out in the wee hours to witness her was not in a position to judge. She drank her Coke with rum. It was less filling so she could keep up with the boys.

Libby nursed the rum mustering the courage to break the news, to the boys, that she had been offered a secretarial position in Minneapolis at a prominent law firm. They were the first to know that she was going to accept. She hadn't yet told her mother or Zach. She wanted their blessing first, feeling that she was letting them down, jumping ship and splitting up their jolly trio. The boys weren't surprised she was leaving. They were more surprised she punched her ticket first. They celebrated her good fortune and promised to search the want ads in earnest.

"I'll come back to visit."

Eddie and Rob knew that wouldn't happen.

She did too.

Reaching for loose change in his pocket, Eddie fed the jukebox and pressed song numbers from memory. Turning back to the table playing air guitar his friends knew what was coming. Their production night anthem had become Loverboy's, "Everybody's Working for the Weekend." Libby let out a whoop and Rob pumped his fists in the air. Their last toast of the evening was to Leland who had recovered enough from the gout to drive the paper to Rugby.

On his way home, Eddie decided to leaf through the type set pages one more time. The front page headline didn't seem right. "Kahl Focus of State Manhurt." He looked twice to make sure he wasn't looking through beer goggles. No such luck.

"Figures," Eddie thought to himself. He fixed the typo and headed for home.

Chapter 9

The ink could still smudge under a thumb when Eddie wrestled a copy of the Herald from the bundles Leland was unloading from his truck. Eddie couldn't imagine anyone having a more dilapidated truck than his. The wheel wells were rusted clear through and the body had all the specifications for a demolition derby.

"Your truck is a piece of shit, Leland." Eddie felt bad after he said it. Leland kept unloading the stack of papers. At his age, it took more than a punk like Eddie to set him off. "My Mercedes is in the garage at home." He winked at Eddie signifying there were no hard feelings and no Mercedes.

Jumping into his own piece of shit with paper in hand Eddie headed to the Tastee Freez where Rob and Libby were waiting. Sneaking a peak at the front page, while negotiating the steering wheel of the truck and shifting gears was a dangerous combination. Not that is was a huge concern to Eddie. There were no center lines on the streets, so proving a case of erratic driving was slim unless he actually veered up on the curb. Anyway, all the law enforcement in Harvey was involved in the Gordon hunt. The good citizens of Harvey were on the honor system.

Rob and Libby were sitting at their regular corner booth threatening each other with the condiments at the table. Eddie bounced into the cushioned bench, tossed the paper on the table tipping over the fries sculpture Rob was assembling between bites. Rob was quick to grab his root beer float before it ended up in his lap. The three of them stared at the front page partly admiring their work and silently searching for errors. Except for a crooked tagline the paper looked good.

"Look what the cat dragged in," Eddie said. Leland had just dropped off a stack of papers at the newsstand outside the burger joint and walked in to order lunch. "Had you cooled your jets for a minute I would have brought the paper to you." They invited Leland to eat with them but he had other rounds to make. He ordered a double cheeseburger to go and was on his way. "Miles to go before I sleep, kids." Before he left he placed one spare copy of the Herald on an open table in the restaurant. It was his own marketing ploy. Those not inclined to share would buy their own copy from the machine outside the door.

Before long there were a few copies of The Herald floating around. Eddie studied faces for reaction. By now the story wasn't breaking news. The casual observer knew who Gordon Kahl was. People still seemed interested and paused between bites of a chili dog to adjust the paper so it wouldn't drop into their glob of ketchup.

"I think we need to go for a ride," Eddie suggested turning his attention back to his friends. His mind was already made up.

Rob didn't like the sound of that. "Where too?"

"What do you say we drive around to see if Gordon pops up?"

"Then what?" Libby wondered. "Make a citizen's arrest?"

"I just can't sit around here watching people eat their lunch." After some gentle prodding and considerable whining, Libby and Rob finally caved to Eddie.

"What are they going to do," Libby thought about her employer. "Fire me!"

"I'm not that lucky," Rob said.

The prevailing view from those in the know was that Gordon had skipped the state for more sympathetic surroundings, slim though they may have been. In a state as small as North Dakota, Gordon's hideout wouldn't have stayed a secret long.

The green Chevy was snug with three people. A quick stop by the newspaper and they had loaded cameras and notebooks. They made their getaway before anyone with more sense could talk them out of it or before someone with more power could put the kibosh on it. Madge watched as their plan unfolded. She was all about rebellion and wouldn't snitch. The rest of the day they followed suspicious vehicles, drove slowly by abandoned farmsteads and generally chased shadows. They pulled over randomly to photograph their road trip and document their day playing hooky. Libby's days were numbered. She was scouting out apartments and schools in the Cities.

"You'll miss this," Eddie told her. Staring out at the baron fields he added, "Take me with you."

They went South along County Highway 3, a straight shot to Interstate 94. A driver heavy on the pedal could cover the entire state along Interstate 94 in five hours. They idled through Hurdsfield, Tuttle and Steele, towns named for early inhabitants. Col. William Tuttle just happened to plat the town and so managed to get it named after him. A lot of the towns were named after military men or developers. Reduced speed signs at the outskirts of towns forced drivers to slow. When they reached Interstate 94 they turned back north on County Highway 30 and into Medina.

Libby spotted the Coffee Cup Cafe. A cup of coffee and a piece of pie sounded good. The cafe had a lunch counter, tables and booths. There were cafes just like it spattered across the state serving hot roast beef and mashed potatoes laden with gravy. They scouted out an open table in the middle of the room. Old men sipped coffee. None of them were Gordon. Though in a town as small as Medina Eddie was sure they all knew him. They were chasing a dead man. Wherever Gordon was the life he had before was gone. No more carving the Thanksgiving turkey, bouncing the grandchildren on his lap, kissing the wife. Same for the slain marshals. Eddie wanted to ask Gordon, "What the hell?" At that moment covering a ribbon cutting made more sense than a story about a senseless killing.

"Where to now?" Libby asked collecting the last of the crust of her pie on her fork.

"I guess it's time to go back," Eddie replied noticeably distracted. Rob had seen this sudden change in mood by Eddie many times before. Most of those times it was after a long night of drinking when the alcohol induced demons would haunt him. The sense of failure dropped over Eddie. Lately it crept upon him without the aid of booze.

It would usually run its course overnight and he would carry on the next day. Rob wasn't about to have travelled as far as they did without seeing the piece of road that changed so many lives. There were no markers, no police tape, no reminders. The piece of road was indistinguishable from any other stretch of road in the state. All the same there was still a sense of sadness.

Rest stops and historical markers were few and far between in the state. There was nothing to capture on film. Black top and grey utility poles. Eddie shot off a couple of reflex pictures. The wind bit at their faces so they did not linger. Not a one of them had taken a note. Huddled back in the truck they drove back to Harvey in silence; tired from the travel and weary of the return.

"What story do we salvage out of this?" Rob asked.

Eddie shrugged. He was tired writing about everything they did. "This one we keep to ourselves."

They passed on beer. Rob had a blind date arranged by Christi Spencer, fulfilling her promise to set him up. Libby had packing to get done and a rummage sale to plan. Ordinarily this would be the time Eddie would catch up on letter writing. Staring at his name-embossed stationary he realized he had nothing to say. Crumpling the paper, he went to bed. A drop of water from the leak in the roof hit him square between the eyes. He rolled over and covered his head with a pillow.

Chapter 10

The biggest news swirling around the Pizza Palace was who sprung for coffee. The morning men's coffee crew played their harmless version of Russian roulette, they dubbed the Numbers Game. Breakfast plates were stacked on the edge of the table and fresh coffee poured. The spirited game revolved around a number between one and one thousand scrawled on a napkin. In turn each member of the crew would call out a number. The loser unfortunate enough to correctly guess the number on the napkin paid the tab. "A lot can get accomplished over a cup of coffee," one of the regulars would say. "Even more over the second cup." The waitress cleared the plates waiting to see who got the bill. Her shift was over and she wanted to go home. The members of the coffee crew were local business men. The farmers had their own group and they tended not to gamble with their money. The coffee break clientele was largely men. The women had too much to do. Morning and afternoon coffee breaks were a mainstay in town and brought calm and order to a hectic day. Venture into any of the cafes at 11:00 a.m. or 4:00 p.m. and there was bound to be someone there waiting to share some fellowship and a cup of java. The Zenith television mounted on the wall in the corner of the cafe broadcast fuzzy screen updates on the trial in Fargo of Kahl's wife, son and Scott Faul. No one in the cafe was paying much attention. They were sick of the attention brought to their town. The talk turned back to the miserable Minnesota Vikings and the miserable weather. Talk of Gordon died off.

Gordon had been on the run for three months. A profiteer would make a few bucks selling "Go, Gordy, Go!" hats. Gordon's luck would run out in Arkansas when he was shot and killed by authorities in a fiery blaze as he holed up in a sympathizer's house. The outcome was inevitable. Stories about Gordon that first captivated viewers and readers became fewer and fewer until there was just a blurb here and there buried inside the paper. Eddie found himself part of the lingering story when a reporter from a competing weekly interviewed him for a piece on how Harvey was coping with the events, the attention and the aftermath. The story comes full circle when the writer becomes part of it. He used the occasion to be complimentary of the citizens of Harvey. "They are hard-working folks," he told the reporter interviewing him. "They pay their taxes and go to church on Sundays." Maybe the story would endear him to the regulars in the cafe.

Gordon had temporarily revitalized Eddie and Rob's passion for journalism. The small town didn't seem so isolated or dead end. They had a renewed pride in their work. 4-H livestock exhibitions weren't such an imposition.

Most of the staff attended the state newspaper convention. Jessica didn't go because she was self conscious about her weight. Madge stayed home because awards banquets were too establishment and political. "Awards are the opium for the masses." When word came that the newspaper would pick up the tab for the meal, Vern was in. He could silence his disdain of Eddie for the weekend.

Randy did his best to persuade his mother what a wonderful learning experience attending the convention would be. He had a speech tournament the same weekend and his mother wasn't about to let her teenage son on any party bus with a bunch of newspaper people. She didn't like him working at the paper in the first place so he knew not to push her too far.

They all piled in the retired school bus rented by the publisher. Minot, North Dakota was host for the convention. Situated 75 miles North of Harvey it was best known for its Air Force base and home of the North Dakota State Fair. Eddie saw The Beach Boys at the state fair when they were all still alive and capable of hitting the high notes. The Minot Chamber of Commerce promoted their town as a destination with the moniker, "Why not Minot?" Most folk had an unfavorable answer to the question. Vern had a commercial driver's license so he agreed to drive so long as he could smoke. The mood was light on the bus. When the bus door swooshed shut the party began. Buses have a way of bringing people together. Its occupants are all stuck going to the same place and no one has a seat belt.

Eddie was fitted for a new charcoal colored wool suit for the event. He wanted to look snappy when he walked up to receive his awards. A tweed jacket with leather elbows hung in his closet, the closest thing a reporter ever got to a suit. Eddie wanted to stand apart from his tweed donned contemporaries so he went to the high end clothing store in town. In the process of chalking and pinning Eddie's suit the haberdasher manhandled Eddie in front of the full-length mirrors. Instead of trying on the suit before leaving for the convention, Eddie pulled the trousers on in the motel room and found the inseam had been stitched three inches too long which reduced his gate to a waddle rather than a stride. He longed in vain for the tweed jacket and a pair of worn jeans that fit just right. Eddie shortened his step and hoped his suit coat would cover up the fashion disaster.

It was a bigger letdown and surprise when the paper was overlooked for its Gordon coverage. Eddie and Rob fully expected validation from their contemporaries. Not even an honorable mention. They bitterly watched The Bottineau Courant carry away a treasure trove of accolades. The group at the Courant table high-fived each other and took turns snapping photos of each other holding their plaques. They were doing what Eddie in his mind had rehearsed himself doing by the end of the banquet. Eddie offered a half-hearted clap but was seething inside. Anybody but the Courant. Four bottles of the house wine appeared at the table. "I figure we still have something to celebrate." Vern was the last person anyone figured would find a silver lining. They toasted each other and celebrated their good work and speculated whether their entries were even submitted by the publisher. Did he discover the severed bass head after all?

"I've been at this paper 28 years," Vern said finishing off one of the bottles of wine. He surprised the hell out of Eddie.

"I've been around longer than any other employee. I bet you didn't know that." Eddie didn't.

Vern exhaled a big cloud of smoke from his Camel cigarette. "It is all I have ever known."

For all of his complaining, Vern had devoted his entire adulthood to the paper. No wonder he wasn't going to let some green horn like Eddie mess it up. Vern had more at stake in the paper than Eddie would ever know.

"It doesn't matter that we didn't win," Vern said passing around another bottle. "What matters is that we keep papers on doorsteps, food on my table and smokes rolled up in my sleeve."

Chapter 11

The Harvey Herald surrendered coverage of the Fargo trial of Gordon's son, his wife and Scott Faul to the dailies. Those who wanted to keep up with the unfolding drama weren't apt to wait for the weekly paper to come to press when other news outlets were instantaneous. The last story of any substance on the Gordon topic walked in the front door of The Harvey Herald. Scott Faul's father said his son had seen a lot of bad things on that road near Medina. Scott was on trial in Fargo for his role in the Medina shootout. The sins of the son become the debt of the father. The man in Eddie's office did not condone his son's involvement, but stood by him as a father would and remembered the good son he raised him to be. His sadness was shared by many in the community. Eddie took notes but asked few questions. This was not about an interview. It was about a father needing to say his peace and restore the family name. When he finished the story Eddie figured that just about everything was said that could be said about that February day near Medina. The trial was just a formality and the outcome inevitable. Security was tight at the federal building in Fargo where the trial was taking place. Armed snipers manned the roof of the federal building. They were there to protect the prosecutors and the accused. There would be no more violence.

Harvey was a long way from the trial. Area farmers were hoping for a bumper crop unless hail wiped it out before the combines could rumble out to the fields. The Farmer's Almanac promised a good season so the mood at the Harvey Farmers Elevator was optimistic. It was as optimistic as farmers get about the weather and grain prices. American Legion, Babe Ruth and adult softball leagues fought over the ball fields. There was a game in progress most evenings during the summer. The field lights could be seen from miles away.

The annual Harvey Fest brought people out of their houses and out on the streets. Food vendors lined the reservoir selling mini donuts, kettle corn and barbecues. The Fest was the annual excuse to join in bathtub races, buffalo chip tossing and chili cook offs. The Chamber of Commerce was banking on their investment in inflatable slides and kiddie carnival rides to attract shoppers with deep pocketbooks to boost their bottom lines.

Rob and Eddie fell back into their old, monotonous routine of grousing and bellyaching. Once again they were malcontents. They scrambled to come up with newsworthy items each week and diced up the community news at every opportunity. The weather was always fodder for news. During the winter months a blizzard was front page. Except for the trudging around in knee deep snow, a blizzard had the trappings for dramatic photographs. What made a blizzard's aftermath harder for everybody else, simplified matters for Rob and Eddie who had to fill the paper with pictures and stories. Each blizzard warranted a story describing how heavy snowfall would delay spring planting for farmers. The paper would be plastered with photos of ladies burying their delicate faces in their knitted scarves, old codgers tempting heart attacks shoveling off their front steps and gloveless teenagers in sneakers pushing cars out of snow drifts.

Libby checked up on them periodically, but as she settled into her new life contact waned. She had left Harvey for good and there was no looking back. From time to time she sent updated photos of Zach, in a confirmation suit, then a football uniform, and at the lake. The surveyor tracked her down in the cities and made all sorts of promises. Once the elusive deadbeat now turned the stalker. Staff mustered up the nerve to ask her out for a couple of beers. They did not hit it off romantically.

"She just doesn't know the warm pipe-smoking, horse-loving guy I do," Eddie wrote to Staff. The satirical words were of little consolation to Staff.

The last he heard she had gotten serious with a sharp-dressed attorney who wasn't scared off by the little man in Libby's life.

The promise of catching a glimpse of a rare comet kept Rob and Eddie out of the bars after a grueling production night. They sat on the tailgate of Eddie's pickup down by the Harvey Reservoir, a pile of empty aluminum cans under their feet. "What is the name of this comet anyhow?" Rob asked not quite convinced Eddie had his information right.

Eddie didn't want to admit that he didn't know. "Does it matter?" He made a mental note to look to it up later.

What North Dakota lacked in scenic landscape it more than made up for it with wide open skies. Except for the headlights from the cars, belonging to kids making out, leaving the parking lot, nothing detracted from the brilliance of the night sky. The comet was predicted to pass near the Big Dipper, an event visible once every 200 years. They saw something flash by and persuaded themselves that it was the comet. They couldn't bear to think that they could have been distracted for a second and missed an event that would never happen again in their lifetimes.

Satisfied at seeing what was there to see, they went to the Ponderosa for a couple of beers and mull over the meaning of life. These philosophy sessions were numbered and yet they were no closer to an answer. Rob had accepted a job in Atlanta as a feature writer for an airline magazine. It wasn't The Washington Post but the pay was good. More people would read his articles from 20,000 feet in one week than would read his stories in a six month period at the Herald. Best of all there was anonymity and no accountability. People in airplanes read as a distraction to turbulence. Dramamine induced coma makes a reader less discriminating.

After Libby left, they had wagered a case of beer on who would punch his ticket out of town next. Not having faith on their own luck, they both bet against themselves. Eddie won the case of beer but would have to drink it on his own. Despite their differences and disagreements they understood how each other felt.

Eddie did not volunteer to help Rob move his stuff this time. Hauling just one piece of furniture to Rob's U-Haul would only hasten his departure. Eddie wasn't about to make it easy on Rob. As his version of a survival kit, Rob gave Eddie a used anthology of modern poetry with a torn cover and crimped pages, Led Zeppelin's *Stairway to Heaven* on a warped vinyl 45 rpm record, and what was left of the elusive baggie of dope. He still would not divulge his supplier.

"Two down, one to go," Rob said.

"I'm never getting out of this place," Eddie bemoaned. "I'll retire with Vern."

Rob thought for a moment, "Each dawn is a new beginning."

"All the books you read and that's the best you can do?" Eddie said.

"How about, hope springs eternal."

"Better."

In a letter to Staff, which happened less frequently lately, Eddie tried to console himself of Rob's departure.

"Rob will be leaving the newspaper. He will go to Georgia to pick peaches. I think it will be good for Rob to get away from newspapers for awhile. As for me, I have little interest in my work here. Mistakes just don't seem to bother me anymore. I guess that is good."

Avoiding the shallow goodbye with the inevitable "lets keep in touch", Rob drove out of town while Eddie was at the paper trying to decipher the notes to a story he had waited too long to review.

Chapter 12

Eddie had all but given up all hope of going to law school. The local attorney had discouraged him from pursuing a career in law. Bill Tobias officed across the street from The Harvey Herald. He placed a weekly ad in the newspaper promising competent and affordable legal services. "There are too many lawyers out there as it is," he told Eddie. Eddie couldn't tell if Bill was weary of the law or just where he practiced it. He would find out firsthand if the law school ever gave him the chance. The clients Eddie saw coming and going from Tobias Law Office all seemed unhappy.

Bill spoke as if trying to persuade a jury. A comment about the weather turned into an argument. He couldn't communicate a thought without becoming a zealous advocate. The glasses on his face were in constant need of adjustment on his nose and he would regularly gesture with them in his hand. Bill had the habit of sweeping the hair from his forehead which, combined with the adjustment of his glasses, made him look nervous and on edge.

Trust me," Bill said. "There are a lot better ways to make a living."

"You obviously haven't worked in the newspaper business," Eddie said.

"I didn't say there weren't worse ways."

Eddie had stopped patronizing the bars and hung up his running shoes. He wasn't getting any healthier but he also wasn't drowning his sorrows in booze. The motorcycle was sold for Blue Book value to pay the bills. Every so often when Eddie was driving to work in his pickup he would see the new owner riding by giving him the thumbs up. Eddie pretended not to see. It was worse than watching a girlfriend in the arms of another man. The glow of the community theatre footlights and the posting of a casting call for the next production was not enough to rekindle the acting bug. He was done participating. He became the invisible man. Except for the bylines in the paper, there was no evidence Eddie was still in town.

He made more frequent trips home for a warm meal and a warm word. In the back of his mind he was hoping one of his parents would tell him it was alright if he didn't go back. He thought the despair showed on his face. If it did, his parents never said a word. There was going home but no staying home.

The change Eddie sought came by mail with postage due. The law school admissions letter came bundled with a stack of overdue bills. The arrival of the letter triggered his spastic colon. Eddie was on the toilet when he opened it. The throne was the best place to be if he was going to be crapped on again by the law school. If the news was bad Eddie had already decided to track down the Navy recruiter. This time the letter began, "We are pleased to inform you . . .", as opposed to, "We regret to inform you . . ." He had to read it again to make sure he was reading the sentence correctly. Eddie would have jumped out of his pants had they not already been down around his knees. Law school would commence in the fall. He dutifully fulfilled his editorial responsibilities. With every ribbon cutting, farm show and sporting activity he reminded himself that soon enough it would all be over.

"I made it Staff! The law school finally let me in. They must have thought that I was someone else. I wasted no time letting the newspaper know that my days were numbered. I've done my time and I am ready to go."

The tea in his cup was cold. The tobacco in his pipe was not drawing smoke. Walking to the kitchen to find a match and heat up the tea pot, Eddie saw his old friend, Isabelle, out the window looking in. He picked out a few ripe apples from the bag next to his back door and went out to say farewell to the old lady. Isabelle seemed flummoxed at Eddie's generosity with the fruit. Eddie patted her mane and held out another apple. She had been a good friend.

On his last day, Madge baked Eddie a pan of brownies. He wasn't too sure whether pot was a secret ingredient. Vern and Laverne seemed way too happy at Eddie's going away party. Eddie didn't know whether it was the brownies or whether they were just happy to see Eddie go. Before he left, Eddie stashed away a few souvenirs; a couple of reporter notebooks, an X-Acto knife and a couple of three inch wooden letters, in particular the "E" and "B", from the old letter press days that were collecting dust in the back of the production room. Nobody would miss them and Eddie thought they would make good paper weights and conversation starters in his future law office.

On the way out of town Eddie drove by the bar that he spent way too much time in and by the church he didn't spend nearly as much time in, as he promised his mom. Eddie had one last stop before leaving Harvey. He pulled into the lot of the Arto's Supper Club and Motel. Babe was his first acquaintance in Harvey and she would be his last goodbye. She was sitting behind the counter half dozing and half watching Fantasy Island on the television. When the bell on the front door announced an arrival she stood on sore feet, arthritic knees and fragile hip and prepared to conduct some business. With eyes focused and aglint Babe motioned Eddie toward her and started scrounging under the counter. From behind the counter she handed Eddie an 1893 Indian Head penny protected in a cardboard sleeve on which her name was written by a hand that had difficulty holding a pen. It was her going away present to Eddie. He was touched with the gesture. The newspaper business had exposed Eddie to a myriad of characters, from all walks of life and labor, and economic and social backgrounds. Babe was one of those he would not have to pause a moment to recall. He was embarrassed that he had nothing to give to her. "You're going to miss it here, Eddie." They laughed. He would miss her. She knew the day Eddie arrived that Harvey wouldn't be his last stop. Careful not to aggravate her osteoporosis, he gave her a gentle over the shoulder hug before leaving. He turned remembering their first meeting, "And you said nothing ever happened here."

The meager belongings he had easily fit in the back of the green monster. During the two years in Harvey his personal assets hadn't increased. He didn't dare balance his checkbook and the only furnishings were his entertainment center and the Lazy Boy recliner. Other than numerous bylines, Eddie didn't have much to show for his time in Harvey. He satisfied himself that at least he didn't leave behind bounced checks like his predecessor.

Until student loan money came rolling in courtesy of the federal government he would again depend on the kindness of his parents for temporary shelter and sustenance. Part of his luggage included a sampling of the newspapers he had brought to life the preceding two years. They were his babies – conceived from pen and film and born on production night. What were before a source of his frustrations were now treasured mementos.

In a month he would be back at school hitting the books and studying torts, contracts and constitutional law. He would be older than many of his classmates, some just old enough to get in the bars and most not old enough to have experienced a shot glass thrown at their head. There was a time and place for everything.

Eddie's mood was high. He hadn't felt that way in a long time. The radio was blaring out the one functioning speaker. He had rolled down the driver and passenger windows to let the fresh air blow through the cab. Pages from a reporter's notebook sitting in the passenger seat flapped in the wind. Eddie held his arm out the window interchanging palm up and down to catch the air. For three years he had written about other people's lives. He had lost track of his own. Now it was time for him to have one.

Aware of the traffic around him, Eddie spotted a Pepsi Cola delivery truck, heavy on the axles with soft drinks, coming toward him. The passenger vehicle approaching on the cross road did not. They also didn't see the stop sign. Eddie helplessly watched the collision—once again the observer. At impact the passenger vehicle stopped on a dime. The Pepsi truck rolled over and landed on its tires. It was a horrific accident, the kind that a fragile human body cannot walk away from. Injuries would be certain and maybe fatal. For a moment, time stood still.

Instinctively Eddie grabbed his loaded Nikon camera from the passenger seat. Old habits die hard. The lens cap was off, the film was advanced and the exposure was set. Coming to his senses he instead reached for the blanket and first aid kit his dad tucked behind the driver's seat. The camera stayed in the truck. The story could wait. The newsman was replaced by the Good Samaritan.

Chapter 13

Law school was painful. Eddie struggled through it, hiding in the back of his class so he wouldn't be called on. He hoped for Bs and settled for Cs. There was no down time. Eddie pined for quiet nights with a steamy cup of Sleepy Time Tea, a tater tot hotdish in the oven and St. Elsewhere on the tube.

Word was that Rob moved to Minneapolis. Georgia was too relaxed even for him. They had gone from knowing each other's thoughts to not knowing where each other lived or what the other was doing. Eddie called Rob's mom to track him down. The unexpected call was her license to extol her son's virtues. She reminded Eddie a lot of his own mother. He reached Rob's answering machine. "Finish that novel yet?" The beep prematurely ended the message before Eddie could leave his name and number. He never called again and never heard back; too caught up in his new life that didn't include the past. They were going in different directions and there was too much distance between them.

Libby transcended the differences. She had made her peace with Harvey and was ready to go back for a visit. Just not alone. Libby invited Eddie to be her escort to the long anticipated wedding of Jay Smith and Christi Spencer. The sharp dressed attorney she was dating decided Libby had too much baggage to help him advance his career. Pages of community news would be written about the wedding. There was even a mention of Eddie being there that did not fall to the razor's edge from the new editor. He wore the same wool suit he bought for the last newspaper convention, though it was a tad snugger than the last time it was worn. It still irked him that they got snubbed at the awards' banquet. People would talk about Libby and Eddie showing up together. "They can just shove it," Libby said defiantly.

Much to his chagrin, The Herald went on without him churning out community news. The paper was still full of farm ads and ribbon cuttings. Vern and LaVerne were making miserable the life of another hapless editor. Even thinking of the names in unison still made Eddie chuckle. He bought a paper and tucked it in with his duffle bag. The urge to search for mistakes was gone.

Eddie and Libby watched the vows and toasted the happy couple at the reception. A table away from them, Eddie saw the angry reader who had chased him through the newspaper. At the bar was the guy who had chucked the shot glass at him. Eddie didn't want to open up any old wounds and the reception hall was too small for all of them. They ducked out during a rousing chair dance. Having paid their respects to the bride and groom, Eddie and Libby were back in the car and drove by the newspaper on Lincoln Avenue. Madge was standing at the counter her finger pointing and berating some customer who was trying to renew his subscription.

"Do you want to go in?"

"I spent enough time there," Eddie said. He peered into the window of the publisher's party room adjoining the newspaper. The fish on the wall was gone, replaced by a sturdy clock. "The yard stick must have given out," he thought to himself.

Eddie had a better idea. He asked Libby to drive to Peaceful Valley. The green monster finally blew up so Eddie had to get a lift from Libby. She was proud of her brand new Honda Civic. The pay was better in the Cities.

The wool suit was too hot for a pleasant spring day. A warm wind blew through the grasses and wild flowers. He got out of the car to enjoy it. Eddie remembered Babe telling him, on his first day in town, that nothing went on in Harvey. Except for that one day in February, she was right. She passed away during semester finals. Eddie didn't make it to the funeral. Babe wouldn't have wanted him to bother. She didn't like anyone making a big to do about her. He still carried the Indian head penny she gave him for good luck.

Rolling down her window Libby called out to Eddie, "You have company."

A few yards away Isabelle was walking toward him, her gait a little slower than he remembered.

"Hello old girl." He whispered, reaching in his pocket for the carrots and celery pilfered from the wedding buffet.

Now, he saw everyone he wanted to see.

A made-for-television movie aired on Gordon Kahl. Not a mention was made of The Harvey Herald. Eddie didn't watch the movie. He was there and knew the ending.

Letters to Staff had become scarce. It was hard to find the energy to write after a day of classes and a night of studying.

When he found a grocer that stocked Sleepy Time Tea he found himself nostalgic about the newspaper days. Waiting for the water to boil, Eddie took out pen and paper. *"Just finished my first year exams. What was I thinking? I should have stayed in Harvey."*

BIOGRAPHY

TIMOTHY P. HILL, practices law at Fargo, North Dakota but is still a newspaper man at heart. He is also the author of *Garden Hose and Ten Below,* a gift to his children and a whimsical look at backyard ice rinks. He and his wife, Angela, raise their two children, Spencer and Ava, at Kindred, a spot on the map in North Dakota "where kindness is a way of life."

DISCLAIMER

The events depicted in *Chasing Gordon* are true. The author was the editor of The Harvey Herald when he was young, had hair and promise. He covered the Gordon Kahl story and far too many ribbon cuttings. Gordon Kahl, Joan Kahl, Yorie Kahl and Scott Faul are all real people. All other characters in *Chasing Gordon* are fictitious or have been embellished upon for story effect. Any resemblance to actual people is purely coincidental.

ACKNOWLEDGEMENTS

I am indebted to my editor, cover artist, agent and good friend, Michael Lacher. Thanks to proof readers Neil Gillund, Patrick Olson and James S. Hill. This story would not have been possible without Ross Kroeber, Rick Lundstrom and Nancy Granner being a part of my life. I want to both thank and blame Chuck Haga and Kevin Carvell for inspiring me to go into journalism.

I am grateful to my parents for supporting me when I decided to go into journalism and supporting me when I decided to leave journalism. Most of all, I want to thank my wife, Angela, and children, Spencer and Ava, who enrich my life and fill the pages of my journals.